GOD IN NEON: STORIES

Sam Slaughter

To my parents

CONTENTS

PART ONE

GOD IN NEON

Ford could feel it coming on like a wave, like the darkness that followed the sun over the mountains. It erupted somewhere back behind his throat in a space not quite in him, but not quite apart either. It had been part of him for the better part of a year now, and had come mostly in ebbs and flows. This feeling of longing had been there for much longer than he cared to remember, but it was only in the past year had he come to really know its presence. Before that, it had almost always just been, much in the way that the hair on his chest and back had almost always been. He didn't welcome the feeling, exactly. But, like an unresponsive dog, he knew he needed to deal with it.

His father sat in a wheelchair by the fire. He had a book in his hands, but seemed to be asleep. The scraps of white hair that were left hung limp off the end of his skull.

"Pa," Ford said. "Pa, I'm going out."

The man didn't stir. He didn't stir much on a good day, but as long as his head was up you could still see the fire there. The energy he no longer expended on moving muscle had, it seemed, was now concentrated in the man's eyes. Decades of memories sat there with no way out. You could see he understood you, but most communication ended there. On the good days, on the days where his father managed to roll himself from window to fireplace, you sometimes got a grunt.

Ford licked his lips. The feeling crept across his tongue. He imagined his father in Vietnam, crawling across the jungle floor. What all had he seen? He never told Ford, even when he could speak. Mud caking in the sun, arm over arm over arm, abdominal muscles tight to protect against everything in the name of God and country. God and country. These days Ford's God came with an ABV.

The older man raised his head when Ford gripped the wheelchair's handles. He turned his head and focused one eye on his son.

"I'm going out, Pa. I'll be back in a bit."

Ford said it without looking down at his father. If their eyes met, his father would know. His father would know the feeling had come over him again. It was only a matter of time. His father had been the one who would bail him out when he woke up on one of the soggy mattresses downtown. He'd done it more than a father should, Ford knew, but he continued to do it regardless. Even after that longer stretch in county, his father had been there. And then, one morning, he wasn't. Ford could still taste the cigar on the backs of his teeth when he'd asked Denton, the one in charge of the overnight shift, where his Pa was. Denton, sized short and squat like a dishwasher, bit his lip.

"Had a stroke last night."

Ford swallowed the little bit of spit he'd accumulated. Denton nodded.

"Had started to drive himself down the mountain and some developer found his car on the side of the road, called it in."

      GOD IN NEON

Since then, almost a year later, Ford tried to keep the feeling under control. It was hard, though, when you had to work and take care of a person who couldn't talk.

Ford rolled his father over to the window. He flicked a switch and the porch light kicked on, illuminating a half-circle that reached a few feet onto the yard. Beyond, there were only stars. Since Vietnam, his father didn't like not knowing. Ford put his father there just in case. If something were to happen, his father would see it. It wouldn't come up on him like the stroke. Nothing would take him by surprise ever again.

The old man rolled his eyes to watch Ford. Ford caught the stare and held it.

"You know I need to," Ford said. He moved over to a set of drawers and pulled out a mess of bungee cords.

"You always brought me to church as a kid, Pa. Told me I needed to have faith in something."

Ford unhooked four cords from the bunch and put the rest back. He ran his teeth over the sides of his tongue. It reminded him of fluffing a pillow, getting the taste buds ready for what was about to happen.

"You showed me, too, that the Lord God wasn't going to help me. If he were, why would I need this? Why wouldn't you still be talking?"

His father stared out into the night. This was how it went. This was Ford's judgment. His father had tried when he was able to stop Ford. He'd slip Ipecac into forties and watch as Ford threw up in the yard. Their hound dog Russ would hover nearby and lap it up. Now, there was just silence.

Ford crouched by one of his father's wheels and slipped the cord through. He'd drilled eyehooks into the wall around the window; now he slipped the end of one cord into an eyehook. He pulled it up to another hook near the windowsill. He could practically taste the bourbon now. He already knew his first drink. Old Crow. He knew it would be a double. He knew he'd be sleeping in his truck that night.

The old man simply looked on. It wasn't Ford's fault that his father didn't understand. His father didn't know the force that pulled him to the bar. It was something holy, something that filled Ford with the light he'd heard his neighbors talk about when they talked about church. They got their light from God. He got his from neon signs. The only people who truly understood that were the ones he drank with. And his mother.

His mother had worshipped at the same altar for years. They found her upside-down in a ditch a decade back. She'd made her choices and he was making his. They understood each other. She'd understand now.

Ford was on the other side, now, hooking the other wheel to the wall. He did it slowly—tenderly, almost. Ford might make it back before his father needed to be in bed. He could try, at least. It wasn't like he did this often. One night in the chair wouldn't kill his father any more than he was already dead. Plus, Ford thought, who knew what the night would lead to? A couple of drinks and the world opened up.

Ford attached the other two cords to the sides of the chair. With all four in place, Ford nudged his father's chair with a toe. It didn't move.

"I'm going to leave some water here for you. You shouldn't need food for a bit, but I'll check on you later," Ford said. Both of them knew there was as good a chance as not that he'd follow through.

Ford set a glass of water with a long straw on the wheelchair's attached tabletop. He put a blanket over his father's legs and adjusted the chair so that it would face the sunrise. Ford clenched and unclenched a hand at his side. He needed to hurry up and get down there. Those drinks wouldn't last forever. He bent down and kissed his father on the forehead. The old man's head smelled of Brylcreem. Ford took a fingernail and scraped it off his lips.

"I'll see you later, Pa."

His father grunted.

Ford imagined the many things that grunt could mean as he closed the door and started his pilgrimage down to the Package Depot.

BLACK MAMBA

Blinky ran the pet shop out on Route 64. There was nothing wrong with his eyes—20/20, he said—but he only had one-and-a-half legs and he said he believed the nickname stopped people from staring at his stump. *A die-version,* he said. I didn't stare at his stump mostly because I'd known Blinky since I was a kid and had gotten used to the fact that he refused a prosthetic. Said it wasn't American. He'd lost the leg in 'Nam, and he wanted everyone to know even though he didn't want people to stare. He was weird like that.

You went to Blinky's pet shop—named Randy's House of Reptiles, for no reason whatsoever, Blinky'd always run the place—to buy shine. There was The Package Depot, but they didn't sell the good stuff. Blinky would never really say where he got his supply from, but *damn* it was good. Real good. You had to buy something pet-related when you went—I usually bought a cat toy, or dog bones for the mutt that hung around the back of my property—but if you did, Blinky took care of you. He was good like that.

I walked into Blinky's on a Wednesday at noon and he was in his usual spot on a bar stool behind the counter.

"Howdy, Ray," he said, nodding.

"Morning, Blinky."

I'd been out since Monday and I was getting shaky. High Life didn't really do it and, by the time I drank enough to do it, I was full and all I wanted to do was piss and sleep.

"What can I do you for on this fine day?"

"I'm needing some dog biscuits. Seems to be coming up on the day I first saw that mutt out back and I kind of wanted to do something nice for him."

Blinky nodded and I crossed the small floor. On either side of the main walkway were tanks. Tanks with frogs. Tanks with lizards. Tanks with snakes. Next to the counter, there was a new tank, and in it, a five-foot-long, charcoal gray snake stretched out under a sun lamp. A sticky note was slapped to the top corner and on it in marker were the words: *Black Mamba, Dangerous*. There was a skull and crossbones under the words. I didn't care much for snakes. I wasn't afraid but, after having the story of Eden drilled into your head as a child, you develop a certain abhorrence. I stood a foot or two to the side of the tank.

"I've got a new flavor in. You should try it," Blinky said. "It's good. Peaches and cream."

He had a smile that was equal parts asylum patient and crack addict. For all I knew—and I never asked—he may have been both.

"Sounds good," I said.

At Blinky's you didn't request things. You took what he gave you and you pretended that it was what you always wanted. You paid what he said and you did it with a smile on your face. Otherwise, you were blackballed. My daddy had been blackballed near the end of his life. The cancer drugs had made him loose, and one day he'd decided to argue with Blinky. Blinky banned him that day and he died three weeks later. It wasn't anything deep like not having shine that did him in. The cancer finally got him. He saw I could handle myself and he just gave up.

Blinky hopped off the stool and shuffled with a cane into a back room. The cops knew about Blinky's operations, but they didn't do anything. Half the force—all two of them—were frequent customers of the pet shop. I'd shared a jar of blackberry with the young Deputy Hill one time, then spent an evening shooting out streetlights. The next day, when someone complained, the sheriff launched a fake investigation to see who had done the deed. They pretended to work on it for a week or two before just not mentioning it anymore.

The snake didn't move a muscle as it lay there. I had heard of black mambas before. The Crocodile Hunter, Steve Erwin, had done an episode on them. One of the most venomous snakes in the

GOD IN NEON

world. Not something to fuck with. That Erwin guy fucked with them, tossed them around, and shouted "crikey" and all that. But Blinky wasn't even close to being Steve Erwin. When Blinky hobbled back to the counter, jar in hand, I asked him about it.

"Got it from a guy," he said, unscrewing the cap. "It's the new market. Poisonous snakes from Africa."

It may have been because I was sober, but that seemed awfully specific.

"Interesting," I said. I eyed the jar. I could smell the peaches from where I stood. My mouth had begun to water and I wanted Blinky to offer me some. I watched him take a drink. His Adam's apple moved in slow motion as he swallowed. He hissed like his inventory. Finally, he pushed the jar across the glass counter toward me. I took it and took a sip.

There was no burn. It was sweet and—damn it—creamy. I blinked and fixed my gaze on him. Blinky smiled, arms crossed on his chest.

"Damn good," I said.

"Oh, I know," he said. "Special recipe right there."

I nodded.

Blinky took the jar back and took another sip. His eyes fixed on the snake next to us.

"Know what that is?" He asked, pointing with the jar. I watched a blob fall from the jar and splatter on the glass. I thought, briefly, of how much he was going to charge me.

"How much you selling it for?"

"Four hundred."

I whistled.

Blinky took another slug of the shine and burped. He handed me the jar back. This was how it went. You never got a full jar, but you got good and drunk before you ever left the shop and you got some good conversation while you were at it.

"I've seen'em go as high as a G," he said. "Four hundred is a discount."

"Who'd be dumb enough to buy one of them?" I took another drink—bigger this time—and handed it back. My cheeks were fuzzy.

"People," Blinky said. "There's always someone to buy something. Just got to offer it right."

I nodded. Watched him drink. I could feel the glass jar in my hands already again. I wanted it there. Needed it. He handed it back.

"I'd never take that home with me. Be afraid it'd kill me at night."

"They're actually quite calm," Blinky said. He hopped off his stool and stood over the tank. He removed the mesh top. The snake lay still. "Ever held one?" he asked me.

I shook my head. I looked down at the shine in my hands and swirled the jar. We'd done a dent in it; I took another big sip. I hoped he had more.

"Time to change that. Like I said, they're surprisingly calm."

With speed that belied him, Blinky grabbed the snake behind the head and pulled it out of the tank. The snake hissed at me and I prayed to every god I'd ever heard of. The crippled man held it out to me. His smile had, if possible, widened.

I took a step back. The snake seemed to have come alive and it bared its fangs. It had a mouth as black as tar—deep and dark and the last thing I'd want coming near me.

"No way am I touching that," I said. "I just came here for some shine, Blinky."

I took another sip as I stepped back again. Behind me, I heard scratching. I imagined scales moving against scales. My head started to spin a little. I remembered a phrase I'd heard on a show once—cognitive dissonance. I thought of that, even though I didn't quite remember what it meant.

Blinky came around the counter with the snake.

"Live a little, Ray. Live a little," he said. "Nothing will prove to you that you're alive like holding one of God's greatest creatures. Think of all of the power that's inside these scales. It's so small, but it could bring down the biggest enemy. Think about that."

I let the thought enter my mind as I backed up. For a one-legged man, he moved quickly. Blinky held the snake out in front of him and I held the jar of shine like a shield. I was about a foot from the door—I knew because I'd reached the fish tanks and they were the first things you saw. Goldfish bobbed in my peripheral. Blinky took another step and, as he did, he slipped. He let out a noise and I watched as the snake flew into the air between us.

I slammed myself backward against the double glass doors and pushed myself out of them as the snake landed on Blinky, who was struggling to get to his feet. The snake hissed once before sinking its fangs into Blinky's neck. Blinky let out a yelp, followed by the word, "help." The snake bit again. I wondered how much venom it had in it and if it would bite even if it was empty.

Blinky managed to roll over and throw the snake off. His eyes didn't look good. He looked sick and I wondered how long he had. He asked for help again. I was frozen in the doorway until the snake started to slither toward me. I held onto one door and stood behind it, waiting till it got closer. Right as it started to cross the threshold, I slammed the door closed.

The snake's head popped off and rolled a few inches past me. The body twitched and blood spilled from the neck. I stared at it a moment before Blinky's yelling brought me back. I opened the door and kicked the snake's body to the side. Blinky was propped against a shelf of fish food. His breathing was heavy.

"Call," he said, coughing. "Call 911."

I fumbled with my cell phone and did as he said. When I finished I sat next to him. He collapsed onto my lap.

"Hide the shine," he said. "It's all back there. They know, but hide it anyway."

I nodded. I felt numb. I couldn't stop staring at the snake's body, still twitching.

"I want to go out classy-like," he said. He tried to laugh, coughed, and stopped. "Real classy."

"Okay, Blinky," I said. "Okay." I patted his head. His hair was greasy.

"You know, I've never been bit before," he said. "I guess there's a first time for everything."

I nodded. I was thirsty, but I couldn't remember what I'd done with the jar that had been in my hand. I looked around and saw it on its side near the door. I must've dropped it in the commotion.

"Can I get you anything?" I asked Blinky.

He shook his head. "Just hang out here, Ray," he said.

Blinky went quiet. He was still breathing, though, and I rubbed the old man's back. I could feel each of his ribs. I listened for the sirens. I hoped they'd come soon, though I knew they wouldn't. I knew we were too far away, knew that the venom had probably started to shut things down. I wondered what it felt like. Was that living? Was that what he'd been talking about?

Blinky grabbed my hand. His own was clammy. I felt wetness in my lap. Blinky was crying. I squeezed his hand.

"Just hide the shine for me," he said again. I'd never been in this position. Not with my granddaddy, not with my daddy. I'd never known my momma. I'd never comforted in death.

"You're going to be fine, Blinky. Just fine. Pretty soon, you're going to be overcharging me for another pint of this fine, fine shine."

Blinky hacked out a laugh.

"You're a good man, Ray. A good man."

He tried to squeeze my hand, it was weak, like a baby. Blinky let go. His breathing slowed. I closed my eyes and prayed for sirens.

NINE SHOTS OF RYE

The bet was made and I couldn't back down.

"If you can down all nine shots in a row, and make your way across the room without tripping or falling or fucking anything up, you will win the Camaro."

Jim set the keys on the bar between us. He'd spent the last twenty minutes moving shit around the bar. It looked like a war zone and, if it weren't eleven in the morning on a Thursday, and if it weren't just the two of us, Carl the day bartender, and one of the older locals—an out-of-work machinist that had gone by Little Tuck since before I'd been born—it might've caused a problem.

But it was just us four, and I had a chance to win our father's pristine 1971 Camaro. He'd had it since the year it was made and had only put 45,000 miles on it. Dan got it when our old man died, even though I was the one who deserved it. I was the one who'd done the hard work. I'd carried him to bed and the bathroom. I'd gotten elbow-deep in his shit when he was talking about seeing ghosts, about seeing our mother—dead a decade. Dan got it because he was older.

I held my hand out.

"Deal."

Dan spit in his hand, looked like he was about to shake, and slapped me.

I cursed and wiped the spit off my face.

"Line 'em up," I said.

I looked at Carl and he set up nine shot glasses on the bar in front of me. His face belied all the questions he wouldn't voice.

"You can't wobble, you can't stumble," Dan said. He pointed at a pyramid of chairs near the middle of the room. "If you knock anything over, the deal's over."

"Let's get this over with," I said. We'd each had a beer already and I was regretting it. I regretted not having had breakfast that morning, too.

Carl poured the shots. Between glasses, he spilled as much as he poured. I hoped Dan wouldn't make me drink that up, too. I wouldn't have put it past him, though.

We'd always bet each other for things. When we were kids, it was candy, the choice of television program, an extra soda. As we grew up, the bets escalated. I'd had to let him make out with my eighth grade girlfriend, Daniela, when he beat me in a hundred yard dash. Daniela dumped me a week later. When we were in high school, he had his car taken away for a month when he took the heat for stealing our father's vodka. He stopped the bets after that for a few months—until they got the best of him again.

The first three shots went down easy. Old Overholt wasn't the best, but it wasn't terrible. In college, I'd spent many nights with a bottle tucked in the crook of my arm, watching Carolina ball games. By the fourth shot, the burn started to flare up. At the sixth, my eyes watered. After seven, I coughed. I don't remember taking shot eight or nine.

When I stood, the world tilted on me. It was not a slow push—like a good drunk—but a violent swap of right-side up and upside-down. I tried to put a hand on the bar, missed. My fist settled on the barstool. I felt warm vinyl and pressed down into it for a second. I had to win this. I couldn't let him beat me. Not at this. Not this time. I'd worked too damn hard on that car for it to slip away.

I took a step and felt my ankles waver. I thought of the word *waver*, followed by *waves*, and stopped moving, hands out at my sides. Somewhere nearby, I heard my brother's ass-bray of a laugh.

"While you do this, I might as well go gas up *my* Camaro," he said, slapping the bar top and laughing.

I flipped him off, licked my lips, and took a tentative step. It seemed some of my equilibrium had come back to me. Not much, but some.

"Tick-tock, Jimmy. Tick-tock."

I couldn't remember if he'd set a time limit, but a deep recess of my brain made me take another step. The part that wouldn't let him beat me again. I managed to dodge one table and duck under two others set up like an entryway without falling.

The television seemed extra loud and I tried to block it out. It felt like the sound waves were throwing me off, I closed my eyes, praying for some sort of reprieve. The door seemed as far away as when I'd started.

I thought about the four-speed transmission. The F-41 performance suspension. The fifteen-inch super sport wheels. All of the things my father made sure I knew by heart. He'd blindfold me and put my hand on a part. I had to know that car inside and out and damn it, I did. Dan? Dan was busy trying to screw whatever fat girl would let him behind the school. I knew the difference between the cool metal curve of and I knew the comfort that was brought on by the smell of grass and grit in the tires.

The pile of chairs in the middle was less of a hassle than I'd expected—I swung wide around them, pulled in a hip so I wouldn't bump the pool cue stand that stood sentry on the side, and continued on. Dan had moved to the far end of the bar. I could see his grin from where I was. His teeth seemed to gleam. I wanted to punch him. I'd always had to do the harder tasks, just to win. What he made me do was always worse then what I bet him. He seemed to enjoy it, too—watching me struggle. Was that what older brothers was for?

Maybe, I told myself, shuffling forward. Maybe it was when you're kids. Not now, not when you're supposed to be the man of the family.

Dan was two or three feet in front of me. He swung a finger back and forth in front of him like a pendulum. He made ticking sounds from the side of his mouth. The grin he wore was nothing less than shit-eating.

I had almost reached the door when Dan stepped in front of me.

"Not so fast, Jimmy. Last obstacle. Me."

He let out another ugly laugh and spread his arms like a basketball player on defense. I stopped short, squinted at him.

"No," I said.

"No? Are you giving up?"

"No," I said again.

I saw the first punch flying before he did. With his hands out, he had no chance to react. I caught him on the nose and heard it crack. He stumbled back and I stumbled forward, punching him again. He fell against the wall; I landed one more solid punch to his clavicle. Even through the rye, my hand throbbed.

"I'm done with this shit," I said. His eyes were wide, but he said nothing. "That car is mine."

Blood ran down his beard and before dropping to the ground in a puddle between us.

"I earned it, so don't act all high and goddamn mighty."

I'd always been bigger than Dan, but this was the first time in twenty-four years I'd been able to use that to my advantage. It felt good. It felt *damn* good. I turned, motioning for Carl to throw me the keys. He did, I missed them, and they skittered through the puddle of blood.

I bent down to get them, fell, crawled to the keys. With those keys in my hand, a feeling of victory came over me. I'd finally bested him. This wouldn't happen again. I sat on the ground looking up at Dan. He'd recovered, I guess, because he'd pulled himself off the wall. His arms were crossed and bright blood highlighted his arms.

"You didn't get past me," he said. "You didn't win."

His boot moved quickly; I smelled the grass and the grit on the rubber sole as it broke my nose.

A SHOT FOR
FATHER STEPHEN

I punched a priest the night I found out my sister worked at a strip club.

I'd ended up at The Titmouse, the only bar open past midnight in town, the night before my father's funeral. I was back in town for the first time in a decade and no one in my family had tried to stop me from heading to the bar. My momma didn't keep liquor in our house on account of my father, but she understood that others drank and didn't kill themselves because of it.

My father didn't die as a direct result of alcohol. It was snake venom, lots of it, but alcohol certainly played a role in the thought process that, one night, led him to believe that he could break into the reptile zoo out on the highway and perform faith healings with the snakes. He'd seen it on TV, my momma said, and the whiskey just got to him. I hadn't been around and I was back for the funeral because I felt bad for that. I was the only one that could've physically stopped him.

At the Titmouse, I heard my sister's voice before I saw her. It was prerecorded, syrupy, announcing drink specials. I spotted her behind the bar and it took a lot for me to not drag her out by her hair. She seemed nonplussed when I walked up.

"What are you doing here?"

"What does it look like, Chuck? I'm working."

I slammed a fist onto the bar.

"Get a drink or get out," she said.

We didn't talk much, and we were never that close, but I still felt something inside that was telling me I needed to stop my sister—even though I knew I couldn't.

"Whiskey. Neat."

I made it through three doubles before my stomach started to relax. I saw people I'd gone to school with, girls I'd fucked, a cop that'd arrested me for breaking into the school once. I ignored them all, trying to fog my mind with sweet corn liquor.

Close to one-thirty, Father Stephen walked in. He sat down next to me. My sister came over and leaned on the bar in front of the priest. I looked over and saw scars sliding under the cups of her bikini top.

"The usual," Father Stephen said. His cheeks were red, like he'd been dipping into the church wine. My sister smiled, grabbed a shot glass and a bottle of tequila.

"Anything you say, Father," she said as she wedged the glass between her breasts and poured a shot. I watched Father Stephen's eyes widen as the golden liquid fell. He clapped like a fat kid in front of a birthday cake and leaned forward. In one swift movement, the priest—belying his age—swung his head back and drained the shot. The glass fell into his palm and he placed it on the bar.

"You smell delicious, as always," he said.

"Thank you, Father," she said. "Another?"

        GOD IN NEON

The word father made me think of my own. What would he do if he saw the town priest taking body shots off his only daughter? I watched Father Stephen take another shot. He missed a good portion of the liquor this time and it dribbled onto his black shirt. It didn't take a genius or a six-pack to know what my father would do.

I finished my whiskey, stood, and turned to face the priest. He wobbled on his stool and when I tapped his shoulder, he smiled up at me.

"Look at this," he shouted. "Two of the Powells. What a delight. Have you taken a shot off your sister? She's quite good at it."

Father Stephen smiled and hiccupped, throwing a thumb in the direction of my sister. She wouldn't meet my gaze. I thought of my father as I pulled my fist back.

My sister screamed and security guards had me by the arms before blood even began to flow. I watched Father Stephen cover his nose. I told him he was supposed to be a man of God. A man of fucking *God*.

As they dragged me out, I thought of my father, waiting to be put into the ground. I thought of all the times he'd done stupid things to stand up for what he thought was right. I may not have been able to be there in his last moments, but I knew—I could feel it rattling my being—that this would make up for it. I was standing up for what was right. That was all he could ever ask for.

BURYING THE JOHNBOAT

Mary stood on her porch with a shovel resting on her shoulder. In her other hand, a tallboy of Miller High Life was sweating in the summer heat. The sun was up and she'd overslept, the hangover punch to the head too much to deal with at seven a.m. when she should've gotten up to send Milton off to day camp. He'd gotten up, though, and gone. Milton knew not to bother his mother some mornings. He'd just eat two cold Pop Tarts and walk the mile to the bus stop where the YMCA bus would pick him up.

The night before, Mary had moved the trailer holding the johnboat into the yard. It sat there now on the crest of the hill behind their double-wide. The dull, green hull sucked in sunlight like a hungry kid. She'd come up with the idea one during of the many nights at the bar, slurping down two-for-one vodka tonics while what amounted to the town's eligible bachelors took turns sliding their rough hands up her thighs. Milton was at home, asleep. He slept hard and long, always had, and she never worried. He had a peashooter to use, if it came to that. But who'd want to break in, anyway? What were they going to steal from her? Her ex-husband's collection of Atlanta Braves trading cards? Go for it. Just don't touch her booze or her child.

Somewhere between her third and fourth of the night, Mary had realized she should do something special for Milton. His birthday was coming up and she hadn't planned anything yet. He hadn't said a word, but he never did, so it'd be up to her to figure it out. Milton loved the boat—he'd always loved going out on it with his father—so Mary had decided she should do something with it. She'd build him his very own play place. Like at the McDonald's out on the highway—but without the other snotty kids that made fun of his Goodwill clothes.

The boat had been her ex-husband's pride and joy. When he'd left, though, he'd gone in the night with little more than his .22 and some clothes. He'd taken the bottle of Johnnie Green Label, too. Mary had always known that when the time came she wasn't going to be lucky enough to keep that.

No one had wanted to buy the boat—a hole had rusted through near the bow—and so it sat next to the trailer for months. She'd sold the engine for parts. Milton climbed on it when he played and Mary always worried he'd catch his foot and cut himself wide open.

The dirt gave way easily and Mary found a rhythm almost as soon as she started. Push, pull, toss. Push, pull, toss, sip. Push, pull, toss. As she sipped, she watched clods roll down the hill. Mary hadn't thought about how deep to set the boat. She stared at the hull and imagined it moving, sliding out of the space in a rain, Milton on board and crushed when it hit the bottom of the hill. She couldn't have that. Mary realized, too, that the deeper she dug, the less of the boat she'd have to see. She imagined that, with every inch she obscured by dirt, one more memory would be forever covered.

She wouldn't have to think about the first time they'd had sex in that boat or the first time they'd gone noodling together or how he had proposed in the middle of a lake in that boat. She'd been so taken then. But now couldn't help but see how stupid the proposal was. How could she say no? They were in the middle of the lake, there was no one else around, nowhere to go, nothing to distract from the situation if she had declined. Mary finished the beer in her hand, crushed the can, and tossed it into the boat. She'd get it later.

Mary worked steadily, pausing often enough to sip that, before too long, the six-pack she'd bought was gone. She'd swing by the gas station before picking up Milton for some more. That'd be the first surprise for him—she'd be there to get him. He wouldn't be expecting that, that was for damn sure. He never said anything about it, but Mary knew he had thoughts about her involvement in his life. She didn't take him to things like his father had. Even at eight, she knew he had those thoughts. Probably the same ones his father had entertained.

After a few hours—having moved onto what was left of a bottle of Aristocrat vodka—Mary had shaved a shallow grave out of the earth. All she needed to do was get the boat off the trailer and she'd be done. Then she could go grab a beer at the bar before Milton got to the bus. That beer was important. She didn't want to lose her buzz. She'd worked too hard for it.

The boat was easier to move than she'd thought. It landed in the hole with a crack and a thump and Mary adjusted its position with a series of kicks. Good. It was in a good space. She stepped inside and jumped up and down, slamming her feet into the floor to help it settle. Each jump sent a vibration into her boots and up through her body. She found her vision slowing, her eyes not keeping up with the movement of her body. It felt good. Damn good. Mary jumped again, pushing down as she landed. She was going to pound it into the ground. She jumped again. It would not come up. She would not have to see it from her porch. She jumped again and again and again as the sun fell behind the tree line.

STUMBLE-RUN

amie Fouts threw Carl Fouts out on the same night that she pulled a knife on him. He'd threatened to leave her—to leave the baby he'd just been informed about—and Jamie hadn't taken it well. Even though they hadn't talked about a kid yet, she'd figured he'd cowboy up. He was the last one in his family line and needed a kid. But he hadn't cowboyed up. Instead, he'd yelled. They weren't ready. They didn't have the money. What had happened to the pills that cost so damn much? When he came at her, she grabbed the knife and held it like a stop sign in. Carl stopped.

She told him to get out, but that he could come back to get his stuff in the morning when she was at work. She was a nurse at the elementary school and spent her days patching up skinned knees and holding pigtails back while girls vomited in her office bathroom.

Carl went into town to The Package Depot, the only bar in town. He had a backpack with him into which he'd managed to stuff his work shirt and a fifth of rum and he sat down on one of the free stools at the bar. Morey and Pat were arguing over the pool table and the rest of the usual crowd occupied the broken-down furniture around him. The Package Depot operated just above cost;

no one complained, so nothing ever changed. Carl ordered gold tequila, double. Neat.

Harry, the bartender since Carl's daddy's time on those same bar stools, slid the drink toward him.

"Where's the missus?"

"Busy," Carl said, downing the liquor. He bit into the lime and spit the rind into the shot glass. Carl coughed and rolled his wrist, motioning for another.

Harry poured. Carl drank. By the fourth round, he was drunk. By the fifth, he was ready to fight. By the sixth—and a bowl of peanuts—he'd calmed down and wanted to sleep. Carl got up to piss. When he came back, he saw Jamie sitting in his seat, a beer and two shot glasses in front of her. One empty, one full. She had a hand on each of the two full glasses. Carl stumble-ran over.

"What do you think you're doing?" he made an attempt to pull the beer glass away, but she held tight.

"What does it look like?"

Someone behind him said he needed to let the good lady drink her drink. Carl shot a middle finger up behind him and heard someone else hoot a laugh.

"I'm going to ask you again," Carl said. He'd sidled in next to her in front of the person on the neighboring stool. He could feel the heat of the man's fat thigh against his back. "What do you think you're doing?"

"Having a goddamn drink," Jamie said. She went to take the shot, but when her hand hit Carl's the whiskey spilled on the bar.

"You sure as shit ain't."

"You can't stop me," Jamie said.

"Like hell." Carl tried to grab the glass, missed, and ended up knocking it over.

"Good enough," he said, staring at the mess.

GOD IN NEON

Jamie hopped up and they stood nose to nose.

"You're an asshole."

"I know," he said. "But you're not hurting my baby."

"So *now* it's yours?" she poked him hard in the chest.

"Just because I don't want it doesn't mean it ain't mine," Carl said.

He stopped a second poke and guided her away from the bar. They stood in the middle of the room. If it were any other night, they would've danced. .38 Special played on the Jukebox. When she went to hit him with her other hand, Carl let her.

"I'm not ready for this kind of thing. You know that," Carl said. "We talked about it when you had the scare."

"It's been a year, Carl. Why wouldn't you be ready now?"

The only answer was one he couldn't use. She'd been abused far more than Carl had been, and she never wanted to hear it when he played that card. She'd show him the scars when he tried.

Carl shrugged. "I'm not ready."

"So then what does it matter what I do now?" Jamie tried to pull her hand away; when she couldn't, she let out a sob and told Carl to let her go. He didn't.

"It matters because that's my baby," he said. He pointed to her stomach. He coughed and covered his mouth to stop bile from coming out.

They weren't moving, but the room spun around him. Carl's eyes felt heavy and he just wanted this to be over. If there was a way to make the baby go away—not go away, but go in reverse— he'd do it in a heartbeat. They'd go back to drinking Rumplemintz and chocolate syrup shooters on Friday nights, watching reruns of *Who Wants to Be A Millionaire* and talking about what they'd do if they ever got on the show.

"Lose," Jamie would always say. "I'd lose right quick."

There wasn't a way to make the baby go away, though, and he'd be damned if he let it live any sort of life close to what he or Jamie had grown up with.

"You lost that baby the moment you walked out that door," Jamie said. She'd pulled away and had started moving toward the bar. Carl followed.

"You kicked me out. You can't act like then when you kicked me out. Yeah, I didn't react like you wanted, like I maybe should've, but you up and sprung that on me like it was nothing."

Jamie shouted at the bartender for another round, Carl stopped him, and Jamie yelled again. Harry looked back and forth, shrugged, and began to pour.

"Do not pour those damn drinks, Harry," Carl said. "She's going to have my child and she can't put that in her."

Someone next to him mumbled something about his momma drinking while pregnant and Carl wanted to hit him. Or show him a mirror. Instead, he closed his eyes, trying to get the world to stop moving. He thought he'd only closed them for a moment, but when he opened them back up, Jamie was chugging a beer. Carl smacked the glass out of her hand. He heard the *tink* as it bounced off Jamie's front tooth then fell and shattered on the bar. Jamie yelled and started cursing at Carl. She had blood running from her mouth.

"What in the fuck is wrong with you? If you don't want the child, then I don't either. Why should I be stuck with it when you're off fucking whoever you please?"

She'd started hitting him again. Carl picked up a bar napkin and slowly pressed it against her lip. Jamie let him.

"I want it," Carl said. It was quiet and he had to say it again so she could hear him.

"Oh do you now?"

Carl nodded. Jamie looked at him, eyebrow raised. Her eyes shot down to the shot glass next to her. Carl saw it, too, and grabbed it before she could. As she moved, the bloody napkin fell from her mouth. Blood ran in the divot in her chin and it made Carl think of umbilical cords.

"I'm going to take every goddamn shot that you try to take for the next nine months if I have to," Carl said. "Will you believe me then?"

When Jamie didn't answer—she was still just staring at him—he downed the whiskey and asked for another. He held it in front of her face.

"I am not letting our baby grow up like you or me. I'm going to make it better than we ever could be."

As he lifted the glass to his lips, he saw Jamie through the golden liquid. She was glowing. Angelic.

BODY SHOTS

Houston called just as I'd set down with a Banquet meal and *Wheel of Fortune*. It was chicken-fried beefsteak night.

"Come down to the bar," he said. He was yelling over music and people shouting. It sounded like a sporting event. "There are two girls here, traveling through, and they're doing shots." He paused. "Body shots."

He hung up without waiting for a response. He knew I'd be down. I knew I'd be down, too. How could I pass up pretty young things and liquor? You don't do that, especially at my age.

I put the meal in the fridge, retrieving the plastic film from the top of the trash and laying it back across the top. In the truck, I listened to Merle and I thought about my own daughter, Michele. I hadn't seen her in well over a year, and last time I'd been so drunk that—I'm told—I called her the wrong name for the better part of the evening. She lived in Raleigh, near her mother. Her mother and I had never married, but we'd lived together and loved each other for the better part of a decade before she'd packed up and left. Said it was the alcohol, said it was my job as a mechanic, said it was eighteen different things that proved to her we'd never work.

There was a BMW in the lot when I got to The Package Depot. It was shiny, new, screaming *I don't belong here*. There were a few other trucks in the gravel lot as well, the locals. Some of them just kept their trucks here because they ended up stumbling home if they were lucky enough to live in town.

I walked in to a round of applause. It wasn't for me. Spread out on one of the scarred tables was a little, blonde girl. She had an empty shot glass resting on her belly button. Above her, a pretty brunette made a sour face and wiped some liquid from her chin. Four or five men were gathered around them. Most weren't looking at their faces. Houston leaned on the bar and motioned me over with a nod.

"They say they're driving through to Little Rock and wanted a break."

The bartender set a Bud down in front of him and Houston held up a finger, pointed at the beer, then at me. "On me," he said.

"Thanks kindly," I said.

Houston pointed at the brunette. "Says it's her car. Daddy bought it for her. They're seniors at State."

"In Raleigh?"

"The same."

I wondered if they knew Michele.

The blonde had hopped off the table and readjusted her shirt before walking over to the bar to order two more shots. I nodded at her as she stood there; she smiled back.

"Going to do a shot? *Everyone's* doing it," she said. She'd leaned over a little and, had I looked down, I'd have gotten an eyeful. I could tell Houston had looked down.

"Maybe," I said. I wasn't really feeling tequila, but I *had* come down here. If not to do a shot, then for what?

Houston clapped my shoulder. "Of course he is. Just let's get a few drinks in him first, little lady." He took a drink from his beer.

"He ain't used to being around such pretty ladies. He needs some liquid courage first."

He backhand-slapped my chest and laughed. I tried to smile. I'd had a few beers at home after work, before heating up my meal, but the little heat I'd accumulated had dissipated on the drive into town.

The girl nodded, smiled at me, and took the shots back over to her table. I heard her ask for a volunteer and a few of the men clamored to be first. Houston finished his beer, got another, and walked over to watch the girls. Jim, the postmaster, was squatted at the side of the brunette's stomach. You could see her ab muscles as she lay there. It looked like she spent as much time in the gym as she did in class. I wondered what her major was. What was she going to do with it after? I finished my beer, ordered a whiskey on the rocks, and sat at the bar.

"They been here a while?" I asked Harry, the bartender.

"'Bout an hour. Looked like they could've been drunk when they came in. Very touchy-feely. Very handsy. The little blonde one gave me a kiss on the cheek when I poured her a vodka cran. Kissed me like it was Christmas Day."

I nodded and sipped, watching. I drank down one, then another whiskey drink. The girls were still at it. They got louder, the men got louder. With each shot, their shirts seemed to climb higher. As the blonde—her name was Paula—lay there, you could see the lacy arcs of her bra peeking out from her shirt. It was baby blue. Everyone could see it; no one complained.

I had a third and a fourth whiskey. I was warm by then, thinking like I never really wanted to, but did anyway. My ex-wife came to mind. She'd never come out with me. Even when we'd been in the same town I'd wondered where she was. I thought about her and my daughter. Michele would be a year younger than these girls.

My phone buzzed and I pulled it out, half expecting it to be Michele. It wasn't. I ignored the call and stared at the two girls. My stomach was warm and my eyes felt heavy and I found myself walking toward the group. Seeing the one girl's skin under the dim bar lights made me want to taste it, to put my lips to it, to taste her. I hadn't been with anyone in a while and seeing her bare stomach reminded me of that. I flexed my hands as I stood watching a young deputy—Hill, I think—take a little long to take the shot. He had his hands on her ribcage and thigh, like he was trying to peek up over it. His fingers were tensed, but the girl didn't seem bothered. She whooped as he took the shot, then sat up, clapping.

I wondered if Michele was somewhere doing this. A frat party, or somewhere else. A dirty bar like this one, letting strangers take shots off her. The last time I'd seen her, she was pretty like her mother and I figured she'd have no trouble getting guys to do this. I felt a twist in my stomach as I imagined my daughter sprawled before me, begging me to take a shot off her belly. Was she showing off the edges of her underwear to a pack of men? Or worse?

Houston nudged another guy to the side and displayed the open space with a flourish of his hands. He spilled his drink as he did so, and I stood on the wet spot on the floor.

It seemed everyone had taken a shot but me.

"Your turn, my man," Houston said.

The brunette looked up at me from the table. I looked her in the eyes, but looked away after a second. She was smiling, but I couldn't do the same. I stared at her flat stomach. I saw the waistband of her underwear at the waist of her denim shorts. Under that, I saw the beginnings of what looked like hair. I must've been staring longer than I thought, because Houston clapped me on the shoulder.

"Are you just going to eye-fuck her all night? Or you going to do the deed like the rest of us?"

  GOD IN NEON

I felt bile rise at the word *fuck*, but the girl giggled and I swallowed the acid. I nodded.

"Ever done one before?" Houston asked. He pointed at the shot. "Just bend over and put your lips around the glass, then pull it up.

"Kaycee here is fine if you use her for," he paused and she giggled again. "Stability."

Kaycee patted her thigh and ran a manicured nail along the ridge of her ribcage. I bit my lip. I couldn't get my daughter out of my head. I imagined her doing this every weekend, giving her body up because she didn't know any better, doing it because she didn't grow up with a good male influence.

I put a hand on Kaycee's ribs and felt her shift down. My pinky brushed against the wire of her bra.

"Ready when you are, Daddy," she said.

I heard Michele's voice, from when she was a kid, telling me she was ready to play dolls. I'd made her a wooden dollhouse and we played every week.

The shot glass rose and fell as Kaycee breathed. My mouth watered a little. My eyes flickered from the girl's to the glass and back. She was smiling, waiting. She seemed like she wanted it. Even if she didn't, I couldn't tell. I really didn't know. I hadn't been there when she'd arrived.

I bent forward. It wasn't Michele that was in front of me. If she was laying out somewhere, that wasn't on me, I realized. It was on my ex-wife. She'd been the one who took my daughter away from me. She hadn't let my daughter have a male role model. She'd been the one who told Michele that I was no good and didn't deserve either of them in her life.

My lips closed around the shot glass and I closed my eyes. As I brought the shot up, I knew that it wasn't that. It wasn't her. It wasn't Michele. It wasn't the girl in front of me or her friend. This was on me and me alone and, as the tequila began to slide over my lips and down my throat, I knew that the only way I was ever going to be able to deal with it was with alcohol.

STEPPING ON THE DEVIL'S TAIL

The doctor told Lilly that if she had another drink she would die. Her organs would stop and she would die where she sat. So if she was going to die, it was going to be at the Package Depot, the only place to sit and drink in town. It was also the only place to buy anything within fifteen miles.

Just the word *drink* made her salivate. Lilly only somewhat believed the doctor. They'd sit in his office staring at each other across a cheap metal desk. She'd wear short skirts and he'd tap his fingers too fast. She lied to him about her drinking, and he knew it, but said nothing. She knew he wasn't getting paid enough to care.

At home, Lilly found the stash of pills that her old roommate had hidden when he was arrested; popped three. The roommate had moved in when her boyfriend had moved out, taking their two kids with him. He didn't keep them, just dropped them with his parents in the next town and kept driving. The parents hated Lilly though, and kept the kids. She hadn't seen them in six months; there were days she woke up screaming for them.

The pills were ecstasy. She sat on the couch watching *Wheel Of Fortune*, waiting for the high to kick in. The doctor had said no alcohol, but he'd never said anything about drugs. Her insides hurt—burned, really—but in a few minutes the pains began to even out, as if Lilly herself was being stretched like putty.

An hour passed, then another. At one point, Lilly popped another pill. It was midnight when she next looked at the clock. Lilly got up and put all the bottles of liquor she had into a box. She caressed a few as she did, remembering. When she was done, she put the box in the bed of her truck, along with the case of Coors that had been left to chill on the porch. She lined them up with the two cans of gasoline that always sat in the truck. The Package Depot would be closing up around now, and the regulars—herself one of them, usually—would be dragging their feet to their cars before driving back up into the hollers where their families had lived in for generations. As they drove in, she drove out of her own holler and down to the bar.

Tom Waits was on the radio. Lilly sang along, her voice just a touch above Waits' gravelly drawl.

"Hey little bird, fly away home. Your house is on fire, your children are alone. Schiffer broke a bottle on Morgan's head and I've been stepping on the Devil's tail."

Lilly watched as the fog on the inside of her window slid away as the heat buffeted it. She passed one other truck on the way down and flipped two fingers up into the headlights. She couldn't see who it was, but the truck looked like it belonged to one of the Dozier boys. If it were Mike, then that would mean The Depot staff were all gone home. Mike worked security and didn't leave until every single drunk was off the property. That was good, Lilly thought, very good.

The lot was empty when Lilly pulled in. There was a car she didn't recognize filling up at the gas station across the street. She waited until the man drove off. Alone now, she got out of the truck and opened the bed. She grabbed two liquor bottles in each hand and walked to the front door of the bar. She opened them and poured all four on the door. She set the bottles down in front of the door like votive candles. Lilly poured the other bottles of liquor on other parts of the façade—the windowsills, along the foundation. It was an old building—wooden—and the siding seemed to soak the booze up like it, too, was thirsty.

When the drinks were gone, Lilly started to toss gasoline on the walls. She felt awake, hit with a second wave of the ecstasy, and the gasoline unfurled in ribbons before splashing against the walls. Lilly sung under her breath as she spread the liquids. She couldn't carry a tune, but she didn't care. The words of "Amazing Grace" tumbled out, mixed with heavy breathing from more exertion than she was used to. When the gas was gone she felt her pockets for a lighter. It wasn't there, so she went across the street to the gas station. The clerk behind the counter, the son of someone she knew from church, was reading. He said it was for school and went back to reading as she wandered the aisles. She looked across the street, but the lights over the pumps reflected off the store's windows and obscured a view of across the bar.

Lilly bought a lighter and a cola and walked back across the street. A car slowed to a roll and the driver spoke through an open window. Lilly stumbled a little and tried to slur her words.

"Just gonna sleep it off," she said with a wave. The driver rolled up his window and rolled off. When he'd turned a corner, Lilly took the lighter out, flicked it, and walked like an altar boy with a candle to the bar door. She smiled as she touched flame to wood. If she couldn't have it, no one would. The flame didn't catch, and Lilly kicked the door. She tried again. Nothing. She cursed, stood up straight and looked around to see if anyone had heard. It was still, there was no one, and Lilly once again put flame to wood. After another minute of trying, Lilly went back to the truck. She popped another pill and pulled out a mess of papers from her glove box. She lit them and touched them to some leaves that had gathered around the foundation. She punched a windowsill that already looked broken and splintered wood from it. She lit those and set them back on the sill. The building began to catch. Flames began to spread. They licked and curled and ate the bar alive. Lilly smiled, leaning against the front of her truck.

It was only a matter of time until the police arrived. It'd be BJ. He always worked the night shift. He'd have coffee stains on his shirt and he'd take her away. That was okay, though, Lilly decided as she watched the building go up. That was okay. She wasn't going to die. Her house was on fire, but her children would not be alone. In the light of the fire, she looked up and said a prayer.

PART TWO

THE GLASS EATER

My company was in Key West for our annual retreat and all I could think about was my father, who ate glass and spit fire here, before I was born. He was the reason I was here, the reason I'd gone for my MBA in the first place.

I'd been with the company for only a few months and had heard that the retreat was really just a vacation. The company higher-ups billed the retreat as four days of team building, reflection, and planning. But "retreat," my cubicle neighbor told me, was code for "do everything you can short of getting arrested." I'd never contemplated doing anything that would bring me anywhere close to being arrested. When I drank, it was mostly alone and mostly in my 950-square-foot apartment.

The first morning on the island, I sat in the Starbucks on the ground floor of our hotel and watched a man dressed in a kilt and a leather vest roll up and park a cart on the sidewalk. He began to pull out little metal sculptures and set them on the cart, hanging a price sign from a two-foot-tall copper dolphin. When he was done, he took a swig from a flask and sat down on a milk crate. My boss, a man who introduced himself as, "Kev, just Kev" on the plane came down a few minutes later. He had a Hawaiian shirt on, barely, and his sandals slapped the stone floor.

"Another beautiful day, huh?" He had a paper-wrapped bagel in the crook of his elbow and two cups of coffee.

I nodded.

"Coffee not getting to you yet? I know the feeling. That's why I get two. Each has two shots of espresso, too." He said it *expresso.* "Can I get you anything?"

I thought of his expense account and asked for another coffee, which he got.

Setting it down, he settled into the plastic chair with a sigh, spent five minutes eating his bagel, then finally looked up as if realizing I was still there. I'd been playing Candy Crush while sipping my coffee.

"It's great being down here in the off-season," he said. "Really love getting to interact with the real Key West folks, not all the tourists."

I thought about saying something about us, but kept a lid on it.

"I've been really impressed with you, you know. You've been showing initiative around the office. Getting stuff done."

"Thank you, sir."

"Kev. Remember?"

"Thank you, Kev."

"I hope this excursion is beneficial to you. I remember when I took my first work retreat. We went to Mobile." He took a sip of coffee. "Mobile, Alabama." He said it *Allybama.* "Ain't much there, if you ask me. We had a hotel bar and that was about it. We ordered more pizza that week than I think I did in all of college." He laughed like I should care. I chuckled.

"Oh yeah?" I said. I was watching a man dressed as Darth Vader outside. He came along on a bicycle with a banjo. Like that was normal. I wondered who was behind the mask.

"I was only a VP when we moved it to Key West. Happy to say that I pushed for it. We needed a new venue, I said. We needed somewhere the company would enjoy going, I said."

I nodded.

"How's your trip so far?" he asked. He pointed his coffee at me like a rifle.

"Good," I said. We'd been in town for less than twenty-four hours. When we'd gotten in the night before I went to the Rite-Aid, picked up a four-pack of Steel Reserve and spent the rest of the night watching true crime shows. "Talking to my wife," I told my coworkers. None of them questioned why I wasn't wearing a ring.

It took another fifteen minutes of pointless questions for my boss to leave. Finally, Kev told me he had to get ready for the day's sessions, and excused himself. He punched me on the shoulder as he left. My father never did that.

A pimpled teen handed me a plate of conch fritters and I took them to a bench near the water. I'd meant to get a beer, too, but forgot. I'd get one when I was done eating. Even in the off-season there was a good crowd gathering for the sunset. People took selfies with the water in the background and tourists who had no reason to buy such expensive cameras tried to take what they considered artsy shots. I was reminded of the one photo of my father that my mother kept after he left. In it, he stands shirtless in striped pants. The ocean and a few islands float in the background and suspender bands hang to his knees. His chest is sunken and dark, like the space left by your feet after standing at the edge of waves. He's not looking at the camera, but up and away. In his hand is a Jack Daniels bottle. People populate the edges of the photo in what is mostly a circle. "He's about to spit," my mother always tells me.

Every fifteen feet or so there was a street performer. Off to my right, a woman with a sleeve tattoo sat on a Rubbermaid tote. She was staring down at her phone and smoking. Most of the tourists had their backs to her while a guy nearby juggled swords. His banter was mostly swallowed by the mass of sunburned people around him.

I watched her sit there. She seemed unaffected by everything going on around her. The sun, falling towards the horizon and lighting the skyline on fire, did nothing, the tourists who snapped pictures of her were ignored. A child, tottering on a six-foot leash came within a foot of her and she didn't budge.

The crowd around the sword juggler clapped and began to disperse. Some simply turned around to face the woman. She finally looked up and saw people coming toward her. I was one of them, abandoning the remnants of the flash-fried conch in a trash bin. When I got within ten feet, I saw her sigh and stand. She reached into a second tub that had been behind her, pulled out a few things, and laid them on the first bin. She pinched her nose and pushed her thumb and forefinger away from the center, rubbing around her eyes in slow circles. She reached down and grabbed a banana from the objects she'd pulled out and ate it, sitting on her haunches and leaning on the tub, tossing the peel into the ocean when she finished. Thirty or so people clapped when she turned around.

"Welcome, welcome, one and all, and thank you," she said, spinning her arms around her in what I thought looked like dance moves from a rave.

"I am the wonderful, the amazing Sister Glass and tonight, before your very eyes I will do not one," she held up a finger, "not two," a second digit shot up, "but three—yes, *three*—fantastical things that will wow not only your eyes but your very soul."

There was a short round of applause. Sister Glass's eyes were locked on something just above the crowd.

"First, my dear and lovely patrons of the arts, I will eat this light bulb." From a pocket I hadn't realized was there, she brought out a clear bulb and held it above her head like she'd just had a great cartoon idea.

Sister Glass invited a kid up to check the bulb. He tapped it with a finger and nodded.

"He says it's real, folks," she said, raising both arms high. The crowd clapped. The woman then leaned over the Rubbermaid and picked up a plastic bag and a small hammer from inside it. She held them up in one hand, with the light bulb in the other—like a very modern Statue of Liberty. I pictured her standing on Ellis Island, the bag waving in the breeze, welcoming hordes of circus folk.

"Normally, folks, I would just put the bulb in my mouth and bite down. But today I thought I'd change it up a bit and show you how the people on the mainland do it."

Someone booed. The woman leaned into it, sticking an ear out.

"What's that?"

The person booed again. Sister Glass shrugged.

"It looks like I won't be acting like a mainlander tonight, folks. Sad, I thought I could be boring for just one night."

More laughter. Sister Glass smiled.

"If you insist, I'll do it the real way."

The woman showed the crowd the light bulb one more time.

"And now, without further ado, I will show you just how bright I really am."

The woman put the metal end of the light bulb in her mouth and bit down. There was a pop and a crackle that reminded me of lightning. The crowd applauded and the woman held up a hand to

　　　　　　　　　GOD IN NEON

still them. She grabbed the bulb in her hand and spit the metal end
out onto the ground.

"You clap like that was the trick? What do I look like
to you? Anyone can bite a light bulb." She held it out to an older
woman. "Want a taste, ma'am?" The woman laughed and shook her
head, a hand covering her mouth.

"The real trick is eating it."

Sister Glass took the broken edge delicately between her lips
and bit down. It sounded like popcorn popping in a far-off room.
It was a slow process, her chewing. It looked like she was having
a seizure, the way her eyes fluttered toward the top of her lids.
She chewed slowly, methodically, swaying her head from side to
side in what I assumed was a way to get the glass to fall where she
needed it. I thought of the beach, of time crunching down the silica
to make the shores. I wondered about her teeth, her throat while
she chewed. How was she not bleeding? When she stopped
chewing, I half-expected her to smile with bloody gums, but there
was no blood. She bent down, grabbed a bottle of water, took a sip,
and swallowed. Opening her mouth and darting her tongue in
and out, she bowed.

"You may also be saying to yourself at this point, 'So she ate
glass, so what?' That's not all that special. Well, you're right. We're
just getting started."

The woman continued to engage with the audience as she
pulled a mallet and a long nail out of the box. The hammer, she
said, was her great-grandfather's. He'd used it to build one of the
first houses on Marathon. The nail, she added, was from Ace. Up
her nose the nail went as she tapped it in. The tapping was gentle,
like a child's, and I wondered if it hurt. I wondered if she messed
up her brain chemistry every time she did it. When she pulled it
out, she offered the nail to a young boy who had his hand out to
grab it before his father pulled his arm back.

"I promise I don't have cooties," she said.

The father gave her a look.

"Now, ladies and gentlemen, what you have all been waiting
for. Me setting myself on fire." As she uttered the last word she
snapped her finger and a small fireball erupted in the space above
her fingertips. There were oohs and aahs.

"You'll especially like this one if you haven't liked anything so
far. Worse comes to worst, you see me get lit on fire, and maybe I

mess up. Street performer well done," she made a motion like calling for a check.

"Do not worry, though. I do have a backup plan in case something goes wrong." She looked over her shoulder. "It's simple. I back up." She made a splashing sound.

The woman dug in the bin and pulled out a lighter, two sticks with tufts of cloth on the end, and a squeeze bottle that should've held ketchup. She lit one of the stick ends, and touched it to the other.

"Some people ask me why I don't use this as my warm-up trick." She paused, but no one laughed. I wanted to, but couldn't bring myself to be the only one. "Nothing? That's okay, I've been told I'm too hot to handle sometimes."

One person clapped. She turned to the woman. "Thank you, ma'am, clearly you are the one with a good sense of humor. I don't know about all these other Philistines."

Sister Glass took the squeeze bottle and sprayed a line on the ground. The fire shined off her eyes. She looked like a jack-o'-lantern.

"Again, do not try this at home—especially if you're hairy."

There were a few chuckles that were cut off as the woman dragged the fire along her pants, leaving a line that lead to her navel. She drew another on the other leg, bringing attention to the crux of the flames. Her jeans glowed in stripes the same color as the sun behind her. In the next moment, the woman leaned over and simply wiped the flames away as easily as you'd dust away sawdust. The crowd clapped.

"I told you," she said, bringing the flame to her lips. "I'm just getting warmed up."

It seemed that every bar I went into, I saw coworkers. At the first, Kev saw me and bought me a shot. I told him I had to go to the bathroom after and left. He was already drunk and I'd be surprised if he remembered seeing me the next morning. In the next three bars, I got three more drinks from older coworkers trying to pretend they could keep up with their younger counterparts—the ones who still measured their weekends in blackouts and used condoms. I'd never had a blackout.

We hadn't done much that day—icebreakers were popular, and teambuilding exercises—but I didn't want to hang out with them. I kept thinking about Sister Glass. At the end of her performance, she'd sat back down on her tote and put her head on her knees. She'd stayed like that, unmoving, for ten minutes.

I wondered if my father ever did that. I thought about going up to her, using my father as my entry into conversation. But by the time I'd worked up the nerve, Sister Glass had pulled herself up and left. Instead, I watched a man and his show pig. "Show pig" were his words. The pig's name was Bullet and he jumped through a ring of fire. The man said if Bullet ever messed up, he'd just change his name to Bacon. As much as I wanted to look away, I found it hard. There was something entrancing about the performers. They pulled you in, made you cheer for them and open your eyes and mouth in wonder like a kid going to the aquarium and seeing a great white for the first time

I'd started wandering the side streets, my path increasingly winding as the shots of whiskey began burning their way through my consciousness. The tourist noises were now a hum behind me when I heard a woman shouting, followed by a man. Then I saw a pig run out from a bar a few yards ahead. It was Bullet, it had to be. How many pigs could there possibly be in Key West? If Bullet was running, then his owner was probably not far behind. The pig stopped at the curb, looking left and right, as if watching for oncoming traffic.

"Here, piggy," I said as I approached, holding a hand out. "Here, Bullet."

The pig turned to look at me and I bent down. It came forward.

"Just like a dog," I said to no one in particular.

"I said get the fuck away from me."

I looked up and saw Sister Glass walk out of the bar, followed closely behind by the guy who owned the pig. Bullet had come over and sat between my knees. I stroked his head; the wiry hairs reminded me of my neighbor's schnauzer.

Sister Glass stopped at the curb and turned around, hands up. I remained quiet, watching. I didn't know these people, didn't particularly want to get involved.

"I bought you a drink, Anita. That means something. You should know that by now. You did the last time."

"Jesus Christ, Adam. Are you *that* pathetic?"

The man, Adam, stepped toward Sister Glass and she pushed her hands out in front of her like she was sending a wave in a pool.

"I said stop."

I looked down. Bullet seemed just as entranced by what was going on as I was. I had heard somewhere that pigs were among the smartest animals on the planet. I patted his head and whispered that it would be okay. Neither of the two performers noticed me.

Adam took another step forward, arm out like he was going to grab her. I picked Bullet up and shouted at the man.

"Hey," I said. "Hey fucking stop, she told you to stop."

The pair turned, two sets of eyes wide as if they had been dropped on a remote island. I took a step forward, holding the pig out in front with two hands. I thought of my niece, how my sister held her when she had a dirty diaper. I wondered if Bullet ever wore diapers.

"Stay out of this," the man said.

"No. Don't you know that you're being a dick?" I asked and raised the pig a little higher. "Stop or I'll throw your pig in the street so it gets hit by a car or breaks a leg or something."

I had no intention of hurting the animal, but it did the trick. The man sighed, his hands fell to his side and he turned to face me.

"Okay, fine, give me the pig."

"Get away from her."

Adam stepped forward, hand out. I set Bullet down. The pig squealed and trotted over to his owner. I walked past the man over to Sister Glass.

The man cursed Sister Glass, she called him an ass-hat, and he turned and left, Bullet at his heels.

After he rounded a corner, Sister Glass smiled at me.

"I'm Anita," she said.

"Dave."

"Thanks," she said. She motioned back toward the bar. "It seems counterproductive, but can I buy you a drink? I promise I won't try and get you to suck me off."

I let out something between a cough and laugh and nodded, following her back into the bar.

Anita—she said that if I called her Sister Glass she'd do what she'd offered to do to Adam and that involved her light bulbs and fire—bought me three drinks. I was good and drunk after the first.

She talked to me about how she both loved and hated performing. It made her feel alive, she said, but it also hurt her.

"I have my masters in anthropology, like my mother, and this is the best I can do. I fucking love amazing people, but there are those days where no one seems to care and you have to work harder just to make your living. People don't get it, don't get what it's like to spit fire, to control things that could kill you."

I listened, nodding, wondering if my father ever felt the same, felt like performing was a curse and not a boon. I had a hard time reconciling that image.

After the third drink, Anita asked if I wanted to walk around a bit. I bought us another round—she was drinking gin and soda—and we started walking back toward Duval.

The tourists were still out, still drunk, and we wound our way through them. While we waited for a light to change, Anita asked me why I was here.

"Work retreat," I said.

"You came here for a retreat?" she asked. "Have you looked around?"

I shrugged. "I didn't pick it."

"What about the people who live here at the end of the world? What's our vacation?"

"Tampa?"

My drink was empty so I tossed the plastic cup in a garbage can as we passed. She stopped walking when we got to the cemetery.

"They bury the dead above ground so that they don't float away in hurricanes," she said, pointing to a mausoleum on the other side of the iron fence.

"My dad told me that once," I said.

"Yeah?"

"Yeah."

I thought about telling her about him, but she started walking again and I stumbled to catch up with her. She didn't need to know. We stopped finally in front of a small bungalow on a low-lit street, somewhere far from where we'd started. What was probably sea-green looked like a worn-out ghost in the dark. Anita pulled a key from her pocket and approached the door.

"Come on," she said. "As I said, I promise I won't make a move on you in exchange for that drink."

She laughed and stepped inside. From the open door I heard at least two dogs barking. My eyes felt hot and swollen. They swam in their sockets; going in seemed like a fine idea.

Anita called out that she was in the back and to walk on through. The house was clean, mostly, and had an overabundance of Egyptian-looking objects:. a miniature pharaoh bust on a coffee table, next to a Great Pyramid replica, next to a photo book about King Tut. The couches were yellow, as was the carpet, and I thought of sand, of being forever thirsty.

"My mother was an Egyptologist, specifically," Anita said as I closed the sliding glass door behind me. A beagle sat in her lap and a lab was curled on the flagstone nearby. Behind her, moonlight glittered off of a half-filled kiddie pool.

"Neat," I said. There was a bottle of Jack sitting on a glass table between us and she pointed to it.

"Guests first," she said. I nodded, took it, swigged, and coughed. Anita laughed.

I looked at my phone while she took a drink. It was close to two, and I had to be up in a few hours. I tried to stand, but my legs wouldn't move.

"It's late," I said.

"It is."

"I should go soon."

She held a hand out. "You've walked all this way. Why not stay and set a while. Why would you walk if you didn't want to set a while?"

I shrugged.

Why had I? She was pretty, sure, but I valued my job. I needed to impress down here.

Half the Jack was gone and my phone had died. The part of my brain that would've worried about that had passed out an hour before. It felt like we were the only ones making sounds on the whole island. Not once did Anita move out of her chair toward me. For my part, I kept my hands in my lap when they weren't around the bottle.

"My father did what you do," I said.

Anita laughed. "Really?"

"He did it here, too. For a while, before he met my mother. I guess he did it after he left, too. Unless he died. He might've died."

"I'm sorry to hear that," she said, hanging her head for a moment.

I waved it off.

"So did you inherit his skill? His showmanship?"

I shook my head.

"So you're telling me you've never done any of it? Not even spitting a little fire?"

"Nope."

Anita leaned forward, elbows on knees and hands out as if to receive a load of branches.

"You're shitting me."

"Why would I do that?" I asked. "You could hurt yourself, cut your mouth open, light yourself on fire."

"Well, yeah. But what if you never had the chance to do that? What kind of life would that be?"

"A fine one," I said, sitting back. Who was this woman to question my choices?

"A boring one," Anita said, standing and wobbling as she did. "Stay here."

She went inside and I thought about leaving. My head had started to pulse and spin. I'd sleep in this chair, walk back to the hotel in the morning. Or take a cab. A cab sounded good.

Anita brought out a lightbulb and set it next to the Jack.

"I'm going to teach you to live a little."

"Pass," I said, reaching for the bottle.

"Anyone can do it. You just can't be stupid about it. You can't just jump in—it's a slow thing."

Anita leaned forward and grabbed the bottle from between my legs where I held it. Pulling a bandana out of her pocket, she placed it over the bulb and *tinked* it with the bottle's base. The bulb collapsed under the bandana like it had been sucked through the floor.

"The key is to go slow. Chew vertically. Don't go in a circle or your mouth will look like afterbirth."

I fought the urge to vomit at the image.

"The last time my father ate glass that I knew of, I was born. Pass," I said. "He didn't eat the glass in the hospital."

Anita didn't respond—she was busy putting different sized pieces of glass into piles.

"You can't have one that's too big or too small. It has to be Goldilocks size."

She selected one the size of a half-dollar and asked me to hold my hand out. I hesitated, but soon relented.

"Once you grind it down, you'll need water. Use the Jack. Again, don't move your tongue, just swirl the whiskey a bit. It'll be sand, basically, and then you'll be able to swallow it."

Anita took a piece in her teeth, one smaller than my own, and bit down. I watched her lips move, her teeth. I wondered how many times my father cut himself, how many times he wondered if this was all there was to life, to living a little. I stared down at the piece of glass for a moment, then opened wide and set it on my molars.

"Slow. Steady. It's how you'll feel alive."

I thought of everything I'd ever done, how it was slow and steady and not living. I wondered what my father was like in his off time. He was never really off around us—always pulling quarters from ears or rabbits from coat pockets. He never stopped. Was family life slow for him?

I bit down and heard the grind and crunch. I held it there like she told me to, slowly lifting my teeth up and bringing them down again. I was aware of every one of my teeth, of every nerve in my tongue, my gums. Thick warmth seeped into the bottom of my mouth. I looked Anita in the eyes. Hers were wide. Watching, waiting. I brought my teeth down again. My blood began to mix with the glass particles. I felt at once connected and apart from everyone who had ever performed on the pier. Another shard cut my gum as I chewed again. The warmth was freeing. It made me think of the sea breeze, of not having agendas, of not having a smart phone. It made me think of my father. I chewed and chewed and chewed.

THE DEAD
RABBITS SOCIETY

Jake found the first one on our daily walk. I was supposed to take him for walks because the doctor said to. So I did, and we were a quarter mile from home when he found the rabbit. It had been hit by a car, and it was curled up in the ditch on the side of the road we walked on. There was a little blood near the nostrils, but aside from that and the bent spine, it could've been sleeping.

Before I knew it, Jake slipped his hand from mine and ran over to the rabbit. He stood above it, pointing. This is what he did sometimes. He pointed. He didn't talk—I was lucky if I got eye contact.

"What's up, bud?" I asked. I walked up and took his hand again. He pointed at the rabbit.

"It's sleeping, Jake. We can't do anything about it."

It was hard to tell how much he understood about death. We'd buried my wife, Georgia, eight months earlier; through it all I had no clue what Jake thought of the situation. Our priest had told him his mommy was on vacation. I said she was sleeping. He cried a lot, but he usually cried, so it was impossible to tell if it was about his mother.

I went to walk away, but Jake wouldn't move. At the half-way point of our walk we usually got ice cream from the family dairy out by the highway. It was a way to calm him down.

Jake stared at the rabbit, pointed again.

"It can't come with us, buddy. I'm sorry," I said, tugging his hand. He pulled his hand away again and squatted down next to the head.

"Don't touch it, Jake," I said. I could see the Ice Cream Hut a few hundred yards away. It sat at the intersection of our county road and the main highway through town. If I could get him there, he'd be fine. He'd get his two scoops of strawberry and forget all about the dead rabbit.

Sitting on his haunches, Jake looked at the dead rabbit. He held a hand out like he was trying to warm it near a fire.

"Jake," I said again. I dropped my voice low, to a level that made Jake flinch.

My son stopped, looked up at my ear, and pointed at the rabbit again.

"We can get you another rabbit. I'll go to the store tomorrow and get you another rabbit. How about that?"

I'd moved to stand behind him. I pulled my flask out and took two quick swigs of Bushmill's. It'd become my other child, that flask. It went everywhere Jake and I did. At night, when I put the flask to bed, I brought out one of the rocks glasses that Georgia and I had gotten for our wedding.

Doctors had told me I shouldn't surprise him and touch him without his knowing, so I waited for Jake to turn around and see I was there before squatting and taking his hand.

He stood. I said his name again. It seemed like it was going to be another one of those times, the ones that every parent hated, where no matter what you did, your child's screams made you sound like you were about to take a blowtorch to their eyebrows. All my daddy would've done was haul off and smack me until I submitted, but you couldn't do that anymore. Especially not with Jake.

I tugged and Jake fell off-balance. He looked at my chest for a moment before opening his mouth. It was like when you got cut— it didn't bleed right away, but once the first bit of blood hit the surface, you had to work to stop it.

Sometimes Jake only had one or two good wails in him. We stood on the side of the road and I waited to see if this was one of those. A car drove by and I ignored what I figured was the driver's stares. Jake continued on. He beat at his own chest like usual, which would've been funny if it didn't leave bruising. We stopped his swim lessons when he started that.

"I'm going to pick you up, buddy, and we're going to go home. When we get there we can put on some cartoons. Okay?" I asked. He cried.

I picked Jake up and held him tight to my chest like you would a cat you didn't want scratching you. I hooked his legs with one arm and squeezed them between my bicep and forearm so he couldn't kick. He was small, but he could do damage. Jake buried his face in my chest as I began to run the quarter mile home. I prayed no one who didn't know us would drive by. If they knew us, at least, they wouldn't immediately think I was trying to steal a child. Jake's moans and sobs vibrated my ribcage, my heart.

Jake wanted nothing to do with the stuffed rabbit I picked up at Walmart after work the next day. He took it and examined it—turning the fluffy white thing over in his hands, an archeologist with an artifact—before throwing it across the room. I brought it back to him a few times, tried to show him that it was just like the rabbit we'd seen the day before, but no. I even sang that "Little Bunny Foo-Foo" song to him, hopping the toy along the kitchen table in time to the tune. I gave up eventually and we watched reruns of *Muppet Babies* until he fell asleep on the couch. I kept a bottle of whiskey on top of the cabinet outside Jake's room so that I wouldn't have to wait after I put him down for the night. After four or seven shots and a half hour of the newscaster telling me the world was going to hell, I decided to take a walk. I went by myself sometimes, when Jake was asleep, just to breathe. I took the same route that he and I did. If I went into the woods that bordered our house I'd probably get lost and that wouldn't do well. I couldn't have Jake waking up in the morning without me there. A half hour without me there, though? He'd be fine. He wouldn't even know. There was once that I came back to Jake crying. He was asleep, stuck in a sad or scary dream. I rubbed his back and cooed to him like my wife would have and he'd eventually calmed down. It was a tip I'd written in a little notebook in the week I'd had between finding out my wife was dying and the last breath she ever took.

The rabbit was still there. Scavengers had gotten to it, though; its eyes were missing. Some of the fur had been ripped off and what was left was stained cotton-candy-pink. I gingerly kicked the carcass off the side of the road and into the ditch. We'd walk on the other side of the road tomorrow, just in case. Jake would know we weren't walking how we usually did, but that tantrum would be more bearable than him trying to pick up what was left of the rabbit. I took my flask out, unscrewed the cap, and poured some on the creature. Not too much, though.

"*Requiem in terra pax*, Fluffy."

◊ ◊ ◊

The Havahart traps were starting to get rusty in the garage. Georgia had insisted on using them to deal with the pests that bothered her garden. She said that shooting the creatures was inhumane. I told her that if shooting them was crazy, than she was living in County Bedlam. It was what we did, what we always did. My first job had been picking off squirrels, possums and raccoons with a .22. Georgia didn't come from here, and she didn't agree with that. She ordered the traps off the Internet—the guy at the feed store laughed when I asked about them—and we humanely trapped and released the little assholes that ate our food.

I hadn't used them in eight months, but I pulled them out and set them on the porch. I filled each of the four with some almost-bad lettuce and carrots and set them in various places around the back yard perimeter. From the porch they looked like glimmering puddles, the way they reflected the moonlight.

The next morning, I had two possums and a raccoon. Before Jake was up, I took my Ruger Varminator with me out to the traps and put a bullet into the skulls of each of the creatures. If nothing else, I'd be getting rid of the pests around my yard. Our garden had gone to shit, but no one wanted vermin around. They were called vermin for a reason. I put the carcasses in a pile about fifty yards into the woods, made the sign of the cross over them, and went back to my yard to refill the traps and get Jake up.

There were no rabbits in the traps for the first three days. In that time I'd bought three other stuffed rabbits, all of which Jake hated.

GOD IN NEON

On our walks, he kept trying to return to where we'd found the first one, and we were forced to turn around, Jake bawling into my chest.

On the fourth day, I caught a rabbit. The pile of creatures in the woods was starting to grow—I'd caught everything *but* a rabbit, it seemed—so it was a relief to see a little, brown thing sitting in the corner of one of the traps. I stood over the trap, staring down at the rabbit, unsure of what to do next. Would Jake want a pet? What did pet rabbits normally eat? The only pets I'd ever known were mutts and the occasional tomcat that killed barn mice.

I brought Jake out to see the rabbit when he woke up. It hadn't moved from the corner of the cage. Jake stared at it from where we stood, three feet away.

"Look, buddy," I said, pointing with my mug. "A rabbit. Like what we saw."

Jake scrunched his face up and shook his head.

"He's yours. Your very own rabbit. We can get him a cage for inside and you'll be able to take him out and pet him whenever you want. You can even name him."

I patted his back and he shook his head again.

"What's wrong?" I asked. Jake pointed at the rabbit and, as if on command, it hopped once.

"See, buddy? He's cute. Let's go get ready for school and afterward we can get him his new home. Think about a name for our new friend."

He wouldn't, I knew that, but the doctors told me to strive for normal. So I strived. I ushered Jake back inside, brought him to school, and went to work.

Jake ignored the rabbit that night and the next day. I had the day off and I found myself outside, staring at the creature. I'd brought a plastic cup filled with whiskey and Coke with me and sat on the sun-warmed grass. I'd put a water bowl in the cage and dropped in a few carrots for it. I named him Paul. I didn't particularly want a pet, but I was willing to try anything. I needed something for Jake. His mother had always known what to do, how to handle him. But I felt lost, stuck. When Jake started to cry and thrash around, the only move I had was to hold him tight until I thought he might suffocate and wait for him to stop. Everything the doctors had suggested didn't work. He wouldn't be distracted by me. He just wouldn't. I'd even tried giving him some whiskey, like his mother had when Jake was teething, but to no avail. He bit my whiskey-soaked finger, drawing blood.

"What are we supposed to do?" I asked the rabbit. It nibbled on the grass at its feet. This was as helpful as talking to the polyester toy. Somewhere, an owl hooted.

"You could be his dinner, you know. This isn't so bad."

I finished my drink, went back inside, and had more whiskey. I'd need to pick Jake up soon and I didn't want him screaming. I was tired of it. In the moments when it was absolutely silent in the house, I could hear him. I wanted it to stop. There was only one option left.

As I opened the cage, the rabbit tried to make a run for it, but I caught it by the scruff. It was soft and I could feel its heart beat through its little body. I grabbed its feet with one hand, squeezed tighter on the neck, and broke it. The rabbit went limp. I held it for a moment, half-expecting it to kick away, alive. When it didn't happen, I brought the rabbit into the shed and put it on the large, wooden work desk at the back. I set my skinning tools on the table next to it and went to find stuffing. The best I could do was balled-up newspaper, some sawdust, and some leftover fake Easter grass. I put it all in a basket and set it aside.

I made little incisions just above each foot and pulled the knife in little lines up the back. I slipped my fingers in and began the process of pulling the hide away. It came off easy, revealing the pink muscle underneath. My father had taught me to field dress animals when I was a kid, and I'd done it often enough that the lightness needed to hold the knife without puncturing anything came back quick. I cut the tailbone and pulled the fur up toward the head. When I got to the head, I cut around the front legs, pulled it up a little more, and cut the head off. I set the body aside to cook up later. I picked the hide up by the ears and listened to blood drip onto the table. I wasn't sure what to do to preserve the inside, exactly, but I figured that if I washed it well it'd be okay. It would be stuffed and, if it came down to it, I could always find another one to replace it.

Then it was time to get Jake, so I took the stuffed rabbit with me in the truck, buckling him into the passenger seat. It sat limp, folding over on itself. Parts bulged where balls of newspaper were and you could see my bad sewing job, but I hoped it'd be good enough. If it wasn't, I'd toss it out the window on the way home.

Jake was inseparable from the rabbit right from the time I gave it to him. He saw it in his seat and grabbed it, holding it to his chest like I held him. He met my eyes for the briefest flicker, then went back to staring at the dashboard and squeezing the rabbit. He didn't seem phased by the rough stitching—I couldn't help but think of my wife and her small fingers, of how she would sew buttons back on my shirts for me because she made a point of showing off her "one domestic" skill, as she called it. The rabbit looked like a misshapen, hairy football to me, but Jake liked it. Later, he sat on the floor and stared at it, and he brought it to bed with him. He threw a fit when I told him he couldn't bring it to school with him the next morning.

"They'll take it away, bud," I told him as he stood in the doorway, crying. It was too early in the morning to deal with this, and I hadn't had a drink yet. I wanted to smack him, I did. Instead, I pulled the rabbit out of his hands and tossed it over my shoulder. I fully expected a call about a meltdown from his teacher before the day was through.

I made sure to bring the rabbit with me when I went to get him. It was weird to see his eyes light up like that. I couldn't remember the last time that had happened, if ever. I'd had the radio off to take a call and midway back to our house I heard what first sounded like the hissing of a hole in a tire. I turned the radio dial down, not that it mattered, and cocked my head to listen. As I turned my head I saw Jake's lips moving. He had the rabbit in his lap facing him and he whispered to it.

"What'd you say, Jake?" I asked, looking at him sidelong. "What's Paul telling you?" As soon as I addressed him, Jake stopped his whispering.

"I heard you saying something, buddy, but you've got to speak up. Daddy can't hear you like that."

I looked over to see Jake turn the rabbit around, like he was letting it see out the front window. I bit my lip and took a breath. If he could talk to the rabbit, he could talk to me.

I'd almost forgotten that I'd kept the other traps out. I was at the kitchen sink, washing some dishes when I saw movement in our yard. I squinted and saw a rabbit in one trap and what looked like a weasel in another. I set the dishes down, drying my hands on my jeans as I climbed a stepladder and unlocked the box I'd built above the back door to house my rifle. I put the weasel down and let it bleed out a bit while I went to look at the rabbit. It was another brown one, a little bigger than the first. It looked up as I approached, twitched its nose at me. It hopped to the side of the cage near me as I squatted down. I ran a finger across its side. If one rabbit made him happy, two had to make Jake happier, I thought. Eventually, he had to open up. Screw what the doctors said. He would. I opened the cage and the rabbit came right to my hand. It was as easy as the first one, and I was done within the hour. I dropped the guts and the weasel on the pile out back. Bodies had been scattered and so the area looked more like a battlefield now. I poured a little of my whiskey over the bodies, made the sign of the cross with two fingers, and used my boot to push some of the dead animals back into something resembling a pile. It had begun to stink something fierce, and as I made my way back to the house, I thought about bears and teddy bears.

Jake was even more pleased with the second rabbit. I'd seat-belted the pair into the truck; when he saw them it seemed like he didn't know what to do. He'd pick one up, look at it, put it down, and do the same with the other. He repeated this over and over until we got home; it took fifteen minutes for him to get out of the car. Jake held a dead rabbit hooked in each elbow. To get him in the house, I did the same to him, holding him like a football. I felt, in a way, like a nesting doll.

I sat on the floor with Jake that night. Behind us, on TV, a baseball game played on mute. He didn't like watching sports with sound, so if sports was on, it was on silent. I didn't mind too much. I had a tumbler of ice and rum nestled between my legs. We rolled a ball back and forth. The rabbits—Paul and Derek—sat on either side of Jake. He'd look at them and hiss whispers. I don't think he was actually talking, but it was more than I got. I rolled the ball a little hard, and it bumped off his knee. Jake looked at the floor in front of my feet.

"I'm sorry, bud. Did that hurt?" When after a minute I got no response, I kept talking. It was best, the doctors told me, over and over. *Normalcy*, they'd chant as I wrote check after check. "Do you like your rabbits? They're pretty fun, huh?"

Jake pulled the rabbits closer. He pet one.

"Daddy is pretty cool for finding those guys, isn't he?"

Jake gave me a half nod.

"If Daddy found more rabbit friends, would you want them?"

Jake nodded. He sat one of the rabbits in his lap. The stitches that closed the eye sockets stared back at me, black thread thick like tree roots. When Jake slept, the rabbits sat on the pillow next to him, staring at nothing. I stood in his doorway, watching him toss and turn a little, getting comfortable after I read him his favorite story. I couldn't kiss him goodnight—he'd never let me— but I watched as he kissed the rabbits each on their foreheads. I spent fifteen minutes staring at the rabbits. My drink had gone watery and I slugged it down in one long swallow as I stood there. I couldn't figure out what about the rabbits did it. He'd seen rabbits before, plenty of them. At the county fair, when he was five, he'd pet one.

The more I looked at his new toys, the less they looked like rabbits. They were horrible little things. The crunched-up paper bulged like tumors, the seams as visible as they were on a baseball. I couldn't figure out what it was. When Jake was asleep, I took Paul the rabbit with me and sat him down on the kitchen table. I refilled my glass and stared at it. I poked it, turned it over and around. My eyelids were getting heavy and I could feel the whiskey, wonderful like a sleepy limb weighing on the back of my brain. I brought the rabbit back upstairs, trying to replace it exactly as it had been before going to bed myself. As I drifted to sleep, I wondered if I had reset the traps.

A week went by with no more rabbits. I'd bought two more traps and set them up in the woods, but had only caught things I didn't want. I'd had to buy more bullets, too. My corpse pile grew. The teenaged girl at the grocery store told me I was going to turn orange with the amount of carrots I was buying. I knew her dad— he was an okay guy, a huge dick when he was drunk, but also a quick shot—so I bit my tongue and didn't tell her what I was thinking: What I did with the carrots was none of her business.

The third rabbit looked exactly like the other two. We named him Joe. I wondered if all wild rabbits looked alike as I snapped its spine and brought it into the shed to stuff. In that quiet week, I'd read up on taxidermy, learned that people sometimes used marbles for eyes and wireframes to help keep the shape. I found a couple marbles in a junk drawer and had set them on my workbench just in case. They were too big, but I stuffed them into the rabbit anyway. In the end, the creature looked surprised and I hoped it wouldn't scare Jake. But he loved it, like I knew he would, and the rabbits started to become members of the family. Jake pulled chairs over to our little kitchen table for them to eat with us—I didn't tell him when we were eating what came inside his stuffed animals—and he began lining them up next to us on the couch, all pointed at the television, all watching without their eyes.

Jake seemed to be opening up, little by little, but only to the rabbits. He still avoided eye contact. I could hear his whispers, but could never make out what he was saying. It felt like building a pyramid. With enough, pieces, I'd eventually get to the top. I'd eventually feel the sun up close. I kept setting traps. Bears must've found my pile, because one day when I went out there wasn't much left at all. I took it as a sign that I could keep going. Nature had hit the restart button.

Two more rabbits, Petunia and Lilly. I went with girls' names this time to mix it up a bit. I didn't want Jake to have an all-male Dead Rabbit Society. My wife wouldn't have allowed that. "Equality," she would've said. Jake would need to interact with both boys and girls.

The rabbits started taking up more space on the couch, the floor. They were multiplying like living rabbits. Jake was in his element. He had even begun to throw less of a tantrum when we walked out the door in the morning for school. If we went anywhere else, we needed to take them, but school he was getting better at. I'd pulled out his old wagon and we toted the rabbits with us on our walks. Five dead, misshapen rabbits pulled along like they were on a royal visit. Every few feet Jake would turn back to look at them, readjust if necessary. I took frequent pulls on my flask.

At dinner, I tried like I did every night to talk to Jake.

"How was school, Jakey?"

Jake moved a forkful of couscous around on his plate, the little balls rolling away from the tines.

"Having a good time with Ms. Rosa?"

I tried a few more questions, to no avail. I finished my drink and stared at my son. He ate, slowly, methodically, and looked at his rabbits. If he wasn't going to talk directly to me, I decided to try a different tactic. I picked one of the stuffed animals up and held it in front of my face. Through pinched vocal chords I asked Jake how his day was. His head shot up to look at the rabbit.

"Did you have a good day, Jake? I'd *love* to know. Petunia and I don't ever hear about your days at school. We're so *lonely* here when you're gone."

I wasn't sure if this was going to help or hurt—did Jake think the rabbit was trying to make him feel bad? I was tipsy enough to not care. The doctors advised against things like this, of course, but were they here now? No. They didn't have to snap little rabbit necks to interact with their sons.

"Come on, Jake, talk to me, I'm a *curious* bunny," I said. I made the rabbit hop in front of my face. From between the ears I could see Jake's eyes following the rabbit. I hopped it again.

"Tell me, Jake, tell me all about school."

Jake's lips moved, but no sound came out. I stopped and cocked my ear to listen.

"I can't hear you, Jakey. You have to speak *louder*." I tried to emphasize words like I thought they would on *Sesame Street*. Jake moved his lips again. His eyes darted to another rabbit, then back to the one I held.

"How will I know how you are, Jakey, if I can't hear you?"

I waited. Jake made no effort to speak louder. I could feel my patience sliding away as it usually did. Even though I'd given up trying to get him to talk to me a while ago, all of my frustrations came rushing back.

"Talk to me," I made the rabbit say. Louder, with insistence. Jake's eyes widened. "Why won't you say anything, Jakey? How can you expect me to like you if you don't talk?"

Jake's mouth moved and a stream of whisper came out.

"Louder," I said. "Louder."

Part of me felt bad, it did, but the overwhelming rest of me wanted this.

"Louder, Jakey. Louder."

Jake pushed his chair away from the table, pulling the other rabbits close to him. He had one on his lap and the rest in a three-point stance around him on the table. He held a hand out. I sighed and put the rabbit down.

"Goddamn it, Jake, talk to the rabbit. Talk to Lilly or Petunia or whatever its name is. How do you expect to survive out there if you don't talk to anyone?"

It was instantaneous. Jake exploded into a fit of sobs and wails and my stomach dropped down into the basement. I closed my eyes and knuckled them. I picked the rabbit back up.

"Jakey, no, Jakey. It's okay, buddy. It's okay. Daddy didn't mean that. Daddy was being mean, but he didn't mean it. Please stop crying."

I stood up and Jake flinched. I rounded the table and went to pick him up. He started punching and I absorbed his little fists as I bent over to pick him up. I held Jake close and felt his tears on my shoulder. I whispered to him in the rabbit voice, telling him it was okay, over and over. Eventually, whether because he'd cried himself out or the voice actually did something, he calmed down. Jake hung limp against me, all sixty pounds of him dead weight. I rocked him, cooing like my wife had taught me.

This was what it came down to. I'd never have my own voice, never have a real conversation with my son. I'd never be able to talk about girls or anything—not that he'd ever have those sorts of conversations. I'd be the voice of a rabbit, and that was it. There was always going to be a furry wall between us. I thought about whiskey and the traps I needed to set up. And getting more carrots.

THE LIGHT OUTSIDE

We hadn't left the bar in nine hours and we weren't sure what time it was. This was one of the few places that had air conditioning and we were content to sit and drink Mount Gay, or sometimes a Banks, if the mood was right. We usually saved the beers for when we were outside, pulling them from an ice chest to keep us cool. There were three of us at the bar. We met there almost every day.

The windows were covered and it was dark. Outside, Crop Over parties rumbled over the reggae thump from the bar's speakers. The bass was something you got used to in time.

"We need to do something," Margeaux said. "Let's do something. The calypso competition is today."

She had her hand on Bruce's thigh while she spoke, but she leaned toward me, her chest almost parallel to the table. I thought about how I could've left him for dead in Iraq as I squeezed my rocks glass and stared at the blade of light under the door. Still daytime. I couldn't remember when we'd gotten here.

"There's also a greased pole competition for anyone to enter," Margeaux said.

Bruce looked at me from across the table and raised a brow. He'd had as much as me, but he'd put on weight since we'd gotten back. My head swum and I was glad for the bar's dimness.

"I'm in," Bruce said. "It'll be fun."

I threw back my rum. "We'd have to drive. I can't drive."

I raised my glass and Erskine, the bartender, came over with the bottle.

"Please?" Margeaux said. She prayed across the table. "Please, Henry?"

I shook my head. It was nice here, and there was plenty of rum. It seemed a much better option than moving about, squeezing between tourists and locals, smelling both body odor and the cocoa butter sweetness of suntan lotion.

"What are you afraid of?" Bruce asked. He'd removed Margeaux's hand and stood, palms on the table between us.

I drank more. "Nothing at all. It'll all be grand. I just don't want to go."

"Then we should," Bruce said. "The contest will be like boot camp. Remember boot camp?"

"Yes," I said. Erskine was nearby and refilled my glass. I'd lost count and had taken to paying lump sums at the end of the day. We all did it. It wasn't a big island,; Erskine could find us if we ever skipped out on a tab.

"Well, we're going, then," Bruce said. "I'm going to win that contest, and I'm going to give my prize to Margeaux."

Bruce pulled her up by the elbow and held her close as he finished his drink. He tossed some bills on the table and guided her out. Margeaux looked over her shoulder as they walked.

"It'll be a damn good time," Margeaux said as Bruce opened the door, flooding the bar with hurtful light.

I nodded. "I know," I said. "I know."

WHISKEY SWEAT

Jake, the neighbor who'd killed Paul's dog, was in the sauna, too. Paul didn't see him at first. He saw steam and the vague outlines of two shapes on the bench along the far wall. He stood just inside the door for a moment, letting his body adapt.

When his eyes adjusted to the dim lighting, he saw an old man with legs spread wide, no towel. The man sat on one side and Jake was taking up the opposite corner. Paul squeezed his fists at his sides and sat between them. In the minute or two he'd been in the sauna, Paul was already smelling last night's whiskey creeping from his pores.

"I spread some peppermint oil," the older man said. "I hope you don't mind."

The only thing on Paul's mind was Jake; he was hoping the old man would leave first. There were no cameras in here, and he doubted the man who was old enough to be his grandfather could see very well in all the steam.

"No problem," Paul said.

"It's supposed to relax you," the main said. "They give it to tigers to relax them, I heard."

"Interesting," Paul said.

The man didn't say anything else, so Paul focused on the door, watching as steam crept up the glass like a virus. He imagined his hangover seeping out of him onto the floor, eventually flowing into the stream trail. He watched the patterns the toxins made as condensation formed and droplets free fell from the surface. No one spoke. Jake had said hello, but Paul had pretended not to hear. He focused on the whiskey sweat.

Paul tapped his thigh. Each *thwap* sent droplets of sweat in little arcs onto the tile bench. His head hurt, but knowing what could happen was enough to make him stick this time in the sauna out.

His girlfriend had made him start coming here—to the sauna and the gym in general. She'd told him it'd help him feel better and that, if he did, she wouldn't ride him for all the empty fifths she saw in the recycling bin every time she came over. Paul'd nodded at the time, smiled and agreed, but only because he'd wanted to have her that night. He'd been through three-quarters of a bottle when she'd arrived, but he'd hidden it under mouthwash and the Old Spice spray she hated. Paul had spent three weeks hiding the bottles, telling her he was going when he wasn't, until she said they'd go together. Now he came because the sauna *did* help, especially when he was hung over.

The steam was thick and stuck to Paul like a used condom. He rotated his neck one way, then the other. He cracked his knuckles. Paul could hear Jake's heel hit the ground as he bounced a leg over and over next to him. It was fast, like a snare drum.

"Guess it's been long enough for me," the old man said. He leaned forward, his back sounding sticky but slick—like a decal being pulled from its backing. He stood up and hobbled over to the door.

"Have a good day, you two," he said, letting in a blast of cold air as he left.

After a moment, Jake went to stand, but Paul put a hand on his shoulder, guiding him back to the tile seat.

"No," Paul said. "Not right now."

Jake shrugged his hand away.

"I know you killed my dog, and we've got to settle that," Paul said. He stood, cinched his towel tighter and stood in front of Jake, who looked up at him like an acolyte to a priest, eyes wide, waiting.

"I did not," Jake said. "I'm sorry your dog died, but I had nothing to do with it."

Jake stood, leaving his towel on the seat. He was almost the same height as Paul. He held his hands up in front of him.

"I don't believe you," Paul said. He crossed his arms, wanting nothing more than to close his eyes—his vision swum from standing too quickly—but he focused on a healed cut just above Jake's lip.

"Why would I kill your damn dog? I love animals."

"You love your tomatoes," Paul said. "You love your fucking tomatoes and when my dog got into them you poisoned him."

Paul took a step forward. The air that followed him was stringent with the scent of plastic-handle Old Crow.

Jake tried to say something else, but Paul held a hand up. His head hurt, and he was done with this. Jake stopped talking.

In one motion, Paul put his hands on Jake's shoulders and brought his knee into Jake's crotch. He pulled down as he pushed up and felt the skin stretch around his kneecap. Jake sat back, coughing. He looked up at Paul, seemingly unable to speak.

Paul looked at Jake and spat on him. "If I see you near our fence line again, I will show you what it is like to bleed out of every pore. Remember Jesus and his crown of thorns? That will be nothing."

Paul had heard his father use this threat once, speaking to a pair of migrant workers that he'd hired to help out on the horse farm from just over the Pennsylvania state line. They'd stolen some extra rubber hoses from a barn. He still remembered how it had affected the threatened. Paul smiled, watching as Jake processed what he'd said. He waited a moment to see if the dog killer would say anything. When he didn't, Paul spit on him again.

FAME IN THE GRAVEYARD

It was just another boring day in the graveyard. We had no burials planned, and it wasn't raining, so there was no excuse to stay in the office with the air conditioner watching *Jerry Springer* or *Maury*. Instead, we—and by "we" I mean Chris and I, the ones that did the hard work—had to pretend to look busy. I did, at least. Chris sat against the bucket of the tractor and smoked a cigarette, either watching me pretending to weed-whack or watching the squirrels in the trees behind me. I couldn't tell and frankly didn't care. I couldn't tell our boss, Frankie, to fuck off for making us work when there was truly nothing to do, either. I was summer help. I needed the money, as bad as it was. That's what happened when you went home for the summer in college, I realized. You ended up digging graves for petty cash.

At about ten, Frankie said instructed us to help dig the hole for a burial the following day. I think he finally saw that we weren't doing much. As old as he was, he was probably bored, too. When Chris and I met him at the spot where the plot would be, a car drove up. Shiny and new, it was the exact opposite of everything around us. I liked it for that. Part of me wanted to touch it, to run a finger along the body like my friends who were actually into cars did from time to time. I didn't know if they got off on that or something, but I had sworn to myself that I'd try it sometime. I would've done it right there if Frankie hadn't warned me multiple times about interacting with people in the cemetery.

"Don't talk to them," he'd said. "Just don't. If they're here, they're in mourning, and the last thing they want is to see your face and hear your voice."

Frankie had known me since I was a kid, and I didn't know how much of that was serious, so I just followed the rule regardless. In my short time working here, there had only been one person I would've talked to, anyway—a girl who had to be around my age who visited a grave that I guessed belonged to her grandmother. She came just about every two weeks. I didn't know her name, so I called her by the name on the grave, Diana Salvaggio. As much as I wanted to talk to Diana Salvaggio, I didn't. If I could, I probably wouldn't have. As much as it sucked to just watch, I wasn't equipped with a set of balls that would allow me to do much else. I could literally put someone in the ground, but I couldn't talk to a girl to save my soul. I was an English major; they called that irony.

The man driving the car stopped a few feet away. The three of us turned and watched him get out. He had a Yankees cap on a balding head. Frankie shook his hand as he walked up, his other hand coming to rest on the man's shoulder.

"Touch," Frankie had told me, "is important in the business of death. People want to be touched when their loved ones die."

"Hi, Pal," Frankie said. Frankie called everyone "Pal." If he liked you, you were "Pally." The man nodded. Frankie turned and told us to hang on, to have a smoke if we wanted. He'd let us know when he was ready.

Chris shrugged and walked away. I trailed a few feet behind, trying to think about the last time Diana Salvaggio had shown up, but I couldn't remember the date. She'd brought daisies. I told myself that daises were the real Diana's favorite flower. I'd remember that. Maybe sometime if I saw daisies, I'd pick them up. Then, when Diana Salvaggio returned, she'd thank me for the flowers for her dearly departed grandmother and start a conversation with me. If she talked to me first, I'd be A-okay. I could do that. It was the starting the conversation that was the problem.

Frankie and the man talked for the next thirty minutes. I walked between headstones in no particular order, feeling like Pacman. I wondered if that's where the idea for the game came from. After a little bit, Chris told me to sit down, I was making him nervous. He was always saying that to everyone.

"Cut that shit out, yo," he'd start, and you knew right then that you were making him nervous. He never explained why he'd get nervous. I thought drugs, but knew better than to press.

I nodded and sat down across from him. He looked up.

"I ever tell you that I hit a guy with a car one time? A beaner," he said, as if we were discussing something as simple as the World Series.

"Oh?" I said. The upturn in my voice made it seem like I was interested and Chris laughed.

"Yeah, the stupid bitch was behind my car over on Broad Street. I was pulling out and he wasn't paying attention and I backed up into hm. It was his fucking fault."

Chris paused to slide another cigarette out of the pack, light it, and take a drag. He coughed.

"I mean, I called 911 like you're supposed to. The guy wasn't dead. But then I left. I didn't need to be there. I had a blunt under my seat, too."

He took another drag.

"He followed my fingers when I moved them in front of his face and shit, too."

I made a noncommittal noise. I really didn't want to hear about how much of a would-be convict my coworker was. I figured when I signed up for the gig that I wouldn't be working with the best and brightest, but that didn't mean I wanted to think about it. There had been another guy at the beginning of the summer. Tony or Tom or something. He was always talking about how he wanted to get away to Nampa, Idaho. He said it was beautiful. He also said he'd be able to avoid child support payments. The name Nampa, when it came out of his mouth, was like a fire siren the way Tony or Tom stretched out the first vowel the way that most people from Jersey and New York did. I didn't do it and it annoyed the hell out of me. He'd never be able to hide in Nampa.

Chris lapsed into silence. I watched a blue jay hop from headstone to headstone, pecking at the tops like they were trays of seeds. Frankie and the visitor kept talking. The visitor's shoulders were slumped and his jacket looked too heavy for summer. I wondered if he was sweating. You could see Frankie's pit stains from across the graveyard.

"I'm done with this. If he wants us, he can walk his lazy ass into the office and get us," Chris said, standing up.

"I'm going to stay out here," I said, "I like the breeze."

Chris dusted off the seat of his pants, flicked the spent cigarette into the grass. He gave me a look, but said nothing as he walked away.

Another ten minutes passed. The cemetery was expectedly quiet. Even the Garden State Parkway, which was just across the fence and down a hill, was muffled by the trees that lined the fences. I thought about all the people, alive, that passed by every day. If you didn't know the cemetery was there, you'd drive right by. It wasn't like the other cemetery over in Newark that was bisected by the Parkway. No matter what, you saw graves. It had unnerved me as a kid when we had to drive through at night on the way back from my aunt and uncle's. I held my breath like my father told me, hoping to ward off ghosts I wasn't sure I believed in. This cemetery, though— this one was hidden. You didn't have to hold your breath when you passed. If a ghost wanted to haunt you, I realized, all it needed to do was hitch a ride, anyway.

More time passed. The only good thing was that I was getting paid to sit around. I had begun to doze, my head dipping against my chest like a fishing bobber when I caught movement in my peripheral. My head shot up. Frankie was waving me over. The other man had driven away.

"Pal," Frankie said. "Go get the tractor. The keys are in it. You know how to drive it?"

Frankie used a checkered bandana to wipe sweat from his forehead. I nodded. He didn't need to know that I didn't. I'd told him I'd driven one before in hopes that he'd let me drive it earlier in the summer. It couldn't be that hard. I'd spent enough time staring at the pedals and switches on the dash while riding on the back of it.

Frankie nodded and sat down on a nearby memorial bench, letting out a whoosh of air as he did. He sounded like a radiator releasing steam. I went and hopped up on the tractor. This was my big chance, my shot to prove that I could drive the hell out of a tractor. Life skill, check. If I did it well—quickly, efficiently—maybe Frankie'd let me drive it more often. I could be his tractor chauffeur.

I took a moment to look around. It was like climbing a mountain, almost. Everything looked different from on high. I'd ridden on the tractor before, sure, but this, this was different. I was in charge. I was the driver. The sound of snapping fingers reached my ears and I saw Frankie motioning for me to hurry up or, more likely, hurry the *fuck* up.

The tractor kicked to life and I breathed in diesel exhaust. I wondered if you could get high off it. I breathed in again, deeper. I wondered if Diana Salvaggio would show up and see me on the tractor. That'd be something. She'd probably be impressed.

The hundred-yard drive was uneventful. Diana Salvaggio didn't show up. Frankie didn't even say thanks. He just nodded and told me to cut the engine.

"We've got to go pick some stuff up from the church," he said. "We'll dig when Chris and I get back."

He brought Chris with him, I suspected, so that Chris didn't do any damage. On one of the days when Frankie had gone to the church alone, Chris and Tony or Tom had a lawnmower race. The build-up to the race was entertaining—trash-talking amongst the dead and bets that would never be fulfilled—but the race itself bordered on tortuous. There is only so much fun you can have watching two machines tutting down a gravel road at five miles an hour. I figured Frankie had heard about it and didn't want Chris out of his sight.

Frankie started walking toward the office. I followed. When we got there, Frankie stood for a moment in front of the sole window. It looked out on the back part of the cemetery, the newer portion. He told Chris they were going to church and stopping at Quick Chek after.

"You want anything, Pal?"

"Gatorade," I said. "Blue."

"Sure thing, Pal," Frankie said, accepting the two folded ones I pulled from my pocket.

Frankie had reached the doorway when he stopped. Chris was out and had started the cemetery pickup already. The big man turned to face me.

"You know that guy I was talking to before?"

I nodded.

"He's out there right now." Frankie pointed out the window behind me. I nodded again.

"We buried his best friend last week and he's pretty upset about it."

A week into my job, I learned to distance myself from any sort of emotion the people at funerals felt for their dead. It wouldn't be beneficial for the gravedigger to be crying along with the family.

"Okay," I said.

"He told me before he doesn't have much to live for and he may have said he has a gun in his trunk." Frankie pointed out the window again. "Keep an eye on him."

I didn't have a chance to respond before he turned and closed the door behind him.

I stared at the closed door. There was a guy who wanted to kill himself outside. He had the means and motive. How did Frankie expect minimum wage me to keep an eye on him? I looked at him through the window. The man stood in front of a mound of settling dirt. His hands were clasped in front of him, is head was down, in profile.

"Don't do it, dude," I said. I knew he couldn't hear me, but I figured I needed to say it. I needed some sort of confirmation that I didn't want this guy to kill himself. There would be no way to get out there in time, even if I moved as soon as I saw him move. And what if he went to his car just to drive away? What if I went out and started yelling and he looked at me like I was a jackass? The man wasn't moving, so I relaxed a little. Frankie was just trying to play it safe. That was all. I pulled a stool over and sat.

I wondered what the guy did. He was probably single, lived alone. He probably had a crappy job, too. Maybe he worked at the movie theater and picked up after all the high school kids on Friday nights. More than once I'd sat in a seat surrounded by the distinct aroma of jizz. it made me feel for the guy, if he did work there. I also wondered how people got away with that.

So he lived alone and worked a crappy minimum wage job. What about his family? Did they live in town, too? Probably not. If they did, he could've holed up there. I continued to stare.

On the television, a newswoman interrupted with a weather update. A storm, the blonde in a tight red dress said, was coming. It'd hit within the hour. Good. It'd clear the guy out. Unless he was into horror movies. A suicide in the rain would be perfect and gory like that.

Most of me hoped he wouldn't do anything. Most. Part of me wanted him to. Maybe not all the way, but at least start to so I could stop him. Even if I couldn't get to him, I could distract him

　　　　　　　　GOD IN NEON

until I did get there. That's what I could do. Then I'd need to call the cops. The local news would find out. I'd be interviewed. Screw driving the tractor, that would single-handedly be the best thing to happen in the graveyard all summer. Maybe all decade.

I could see the headlines. *Home for summer, local man saves another. Virgin Mary School Alumnus a Hero. No time for panic for local man. A grave situation at Mount Olive Cemetery.* The newspapers would be all over it. The New York stations would probably send someone out. I could be on the five o'clock news. I'd be a hero.

A knock startled me. I coughed and turned around. I coughed again when I saw that it was Diana Salvaggio. The Diana Salvaggio. The alive one, at least. Her hand was still in a fist against the doorframe. I gave a smile, which she reciprocated. I couldn't tell if she recognized me.

"Daises," I said.

"Daises?"

"Diana."

I held up a hand and squeezed my eyes shut for a second. I was going to blow it and I had only said two words.

"Sorry," I said. "Hello. You bring daises normally. That's how I know who you are. You visit the Salvaggio plot."

She paused a moment before nodding. "My grandmother always liked them. I'm the only one in the area still. My parents moved down to Toms River."

"Nice," I said.

She shrugged. "I'm Nicole."

"Tyler," I said. She held out a hand and I shook it. Smooth skin, soft, just like I'd imagined.

"How can I help you?"

I hoped it was nothing. The sum total of my capabilities was weed-whacking and trash pickup. I could handle week-dead flowers without vomiting on them. I could wield a shovel like a beast and move dirt, but I didn't think she'd need that.

"I just wanted to let you know that it looks like there's animals eating some of the flowers on my grandmother's grave and some of the other ones. Is there anything you can do about that?"

I shrugged. "Not really. Deer get in somehow over the fence. And then there are rats and possums and raccoons and everything. They tend to come out at night."

"I see. Is there any kind of stuff you can spray on the flowers? Insecticide or pest repellent or anything?"

"Sorry, can you hold on one second?" I asked as I turned back to the window. The guy was still there. I wondered if he had moved at all.

"What was that?" Nicole raised an eyebrow.

"Nothing," I said. "I just had to check something out."

She gave me the same smirk a couple of cheerleaders had given me the one time in high school when I'd tried to talk to them at lunch.

"Really, it was nothing. I just had to check something. I'm in charge right now," I puffed up my chest a little, trying to not make it obvious. "I just had to check something."

I threw a thumb over my shoulder at the window then brought it back and held it in my other hand. I squeezed.

Brain vomit, my mind was telling me, *you're speaking brain vomit.*

Nicole took a step forward. "What are you checking on? No one is going anywhere."

"Nothing," I said. I stepped back. I could smell her on the little breeze she pushed into the space between us. She smelled like what I imagined Victoria's Secret smelled like.

Nicole crossed her arms and leaned to the side, looking past my head and out the window. She shrugged, straightened, and remained in place. I contemplated telling her about the guy. If I did, she might freak out. She could run out there and try to preemptively stop him and that wouldn't end well for anyone. If she didn't freak out, and something happened, I'd have to share the press coverage with her. We'd be in it together. I went back and forth in my head about that. We'd be in it together. In pictures. I could comfort her. She'd take solace in nuzzling into my shoulder. I practically felt her hair under my chin already.

"There's a guy out there," I said. "That's all. He's having a tough time and my boss told me I needed to look after him." I paused. "Just in case."

"Just in case what?" Nicole asked as she brushed past me and stood in front of the window. Her head moved left and right before

GOD IN NEON

seeing the man. I wondered if he had moved and I also wondered if she knew him. If she did, that could maybe make things easier.

I didn't say anything. The crowd on *Maury* was heckling someone on stage. I looked at the screen quickly—when I looked back, Nicole had turned around. She raised her eyebrows.

"In case," I said. "You know. In case he tries to off himself."

How were you supposed to talk about that? Did you say "kill" or "off" or what? What was the proper parlance?"

"Does that happen a lot here?"

I shook my head.

"Should you maybe stop him?" Nicole moved back toward the door. I caught another whiff of her.

"What if he isn't going to do anything?"

"Would you want to be the one that has to clean that up if he did?"

I had let her in on part of what was going on. Did I tell her about my plan that involved me not cleaning up anything but awards?

"I just don't want to scare him. Like a deer, you know? Sometimes its better to not move and just let things happen. Let the deer graze.

"So you're saying the guy is the same as a deer?" Her voice wasn't angry, but it wasn't not.

"Sort of."

"I see."

I bent one knee, then the other. What was I supposed to do now? Nicole didn't seem to be leaving and I wanted to go back to watching the guy. I'd had my moment with the girl I'd thought about all summer and it was not nearly as good as I thought it'd be. I just wanted to watch that guy. Just in case. We passed a minute in silence. What did she want from me?

She swayed as she stood, looking over me out the window every few seconds. It looked like she was trying to decide something.

"Well, if you have to watch him, why are you in here? What if something does happen? You wouldn't be able to get to him in time."

She had a point, one I hadn't considered, but I could tell it wasn't coming from the same place I was thinking. I shrugged and she grabbed my hand.

"Come on," she said. "Let's go outside and watch."

I followed her out and around the corner. We stood fifty yards away under the shade of an alder. The man, if paler, could've passed as a statue, casting his silhouette on the dirt pile in front of him.

"How long has he been here?" Nicole asked in a whisper. She'd sat down on a nearby headstone.

"A little over an hour." I sat on a headstone next to her. *Thanks*, I said in my head to the Donaldson family. "Did you know it's illegal to take a picture of a head stone if you can see the name unless you have the family's consent?"

"I did not. Got any other interesting facts?"

I wanted desperately to know why she was sticking around, but I was supposed to be asking questions, not seeking answers.

"They used to not bury babies in caskets. Just in cloth or something."

"Creepy," she said. I nodded.

"How did you get this job?" she asked. I told her about being home for the summer from college. She told me it was a neat place to work. I told her it was quiet. She told me she worked at the A&P and it was not in the least bit interesting.

"Once in a while a senior citizen slips and falls, but you can't laugh. You need to cordon off the area and pretend it isn't funny that they may have actually slipped on a banana peel or something. The produce aisles are where it typically happens."

Nicole kept her eyes on the man as she talked, like he was a zoo creature. I'd grown bored with watching. Nothing was going to happen, I decided. If he was going to, he would've by now.

"How do you know his intentions?" Nicole asked.

"My boss told me. They talked for a while before he went to his friend's plot."

"Do you think he'll do anything?"

I shook my head.

"Damn," she said. I turned and Nicole laughed.

"You *want* him to do something?"

"Do I want him dead? No, of course not. Do I want something to happen? Yes, yes I do. This town is small and boring. Anything happening is a good thing."

I bit my lip at looked at the guy. She was just like me. I squinted and tried to will him to move. If she wanted something to

GOD IN NEON

happen, I wanted to be the one to make it happen. And then stop it from happening. This could be it. Nicole wanted me to be a hero as much as *I* wanted to *be* the hero. My fists rested against my thighs and I squeezed tight. I tensed my toes in my boots. I did everything I could without moving to try and communicate to the man's back that he needed to do something. I pressed into the ground. I could feel a yell sitting in my throat. This would be my moment.

The man, I could see it, would straighten and without looking up move toward his car. I'd be off then, yelling. "Don't do it!" and, "You've got too much to live for!" Everything from the movies. I imagined tackling him to the ground as he reached into the trunk. Nicole would swoon.

I wanted the man to move. There was too much at stake for him not to. He needed to do this. Wasn't that what being a good person was about? Sacrifice?

Nicole touched my shoulder and I startled.

"Are you okay? You look like you're having a heart attack."

"Fine," I said. I wondered if she could see my heart pounding. "I'm fine."

At that moment the man let out a sob. He moved a hand to cover his face. I stood.

"He's going to do it," I said. I felt it. "I've got to stop him."

Nicole made a grab for my arm, but I was off at a trot already, dodging tombstones like a Heisman winner. I was in the zone and didn't hear whatever Nicole said as I took off.

The man had just about made it to the trunk of his car when I clipped the edge of a black, marble tombstone. I hit the ground with a thud. The guy looked in my direction for a moment before turning back to his car and opening the trunk. I pushed myself to my knees. I was running out of time. Who knew how long it would take him to get the gun? Would there be any sort of ceremony before pulling the trigger? I looked back at where Nicole was, except she wasn't there. I spun to try and locate her. Why wasn't she there to see my moment in the sun? Who was going to let the cops know about my heroism besides me?

The man was leaning into his trunk. Everything seemed to be happening slower. Would the gun shine? What kind of gun was it? Had Frankie said? Even if Nicole wasn't there, I'd need to do this. The man straightened and brought a water bottle to his lips. He drank half, capped it, and dropped it back into the trunk.

No gun, no shot, no suicide. Water. Hydration. That was all it was. The man opened his door, got in, and drove off. I don't know if he knew I was even there. I spun in another circle. Nicole was nowhere. I cursed and kicked a headstone, then immediately apologized to the family.

I sat down on the gravel road. The guy had left and so had Nicole. I hadn't even given her the daisies I'd picked off the Tasco plot and stored in the fridge.

Somewhere outside the cemetery, an ice cream truck bleated its tune. The tune made me think of the shore, where my mother had snapped pictures of me every summer, bathing suit always a size too big. Ice cream usually half-melted on my face and the beach blanket. Those pictures were all over my parents' house. People commented on them whenever they came over. Maybe, I thought, maybe that was all the fame I needed.

FROZEN JONAS

"**G**et up," Jacky said.

She tossed a boot at Tim, who'd been passed out on the couch for an hour. She stood in the doorway in her ski jacket and hat with the tassels that he said made her look like Pippi Longstocking. The boot landed squarely on Tim's stomach, pushing the air out like a pool toy being deflated at the end of summer.

"I'm up," he said, sitting up to put the boot on. He motioned for her to toss the other one. "Why am I am up?"

"Jonas is gone."

Tim usually left Jonas, the mutt Jacky had brought home six months earlier, outside during the day while she was at work. Fresh air and sunshine, he'd tell himself over the top of a bottle.

"He's in the yard," Tim said.

He'd joined Jacky by the apartment door and was pulling on a ratty fleece sweatshirt. Tim stood and blinked—first one eye, then the other, then both. He picked at a crust that had formed in his eyelashes.

"No, he's not. He's gone," Jacky said. "Let's go. We need to find him."

She hooked a finger through a hole in his sleeve and pulled him down the stairs and through the front door that never locked.

"I left him tied up after he shit," Tim said. His boots clopped like a rubber horseshoes on the sidewalk.

In the car, Jacky rolled down the windows. It was December in New Hampshire, but when Tim tried to roll the window up, Jacky engaged the child lock.

"No," she said. "You smell. You always smell. Like sweaty beer. Our apartment smells like sweaty beer." She paused. "I sometimes wonder when the last time was that you actually sweat real sweat."

Tim sniffed. The air *did* have the vague aroma of a dive bar. Jacky switched between staring out the front and driver side windows. Tim faced ahead, blinking. He shook his head and tried to crack his neck. He flexed his fingers. He sighed, then farted.

"Look for Jonas," Jacky said.

"How are we going to find him? We live in a fucking city," Tim said. "I mean, are we going to drive up and down every damn alley? One of those little hood rats is probably trying to sell Jonas for crack money."

Tim heard the smack to the side of his thigh, but didn't feel it. Jacky told him to turn his fucking body and look out the fucking window. If he saw anything, he needed to open his fucking mouth.

The radio was off and they were left with the crunch of tires on snow crust and rock salt. Jacky worked her way through their neighborhood's grid system. She rolled along, the speedometer never creeping over ten. Except for tapping her fingers on the top of the steering wheel, Jacky was silent. Her eyebrows were bunched, perhaps because of the—sun glaring violently off of snow. Or maybe it was something else. Tim couldn't decide.

"Where are your sunglasses?" Tim asked. He opened the glove compartment, letting registration papers and the owner's manual spill out onto his feet. When Jacky didn't answer, Tim stuffed the papers back into the compartment and shut it.

Tim stared out the window. He felt the tip of his nose relenting to the weather. Somali refugees sat on their stoops in brightly-dyed dresses and thrift store parkas. Shopping carts sat abandoned, at least one every block—some were flipped like animal traps, some sat collecting snow. Tim thought of summertime, how the kids would run up and down the block yelling with carts, because they weren't in school and because they didn't know there were better things than shopping carts.

He didn't see the dog.

A few blocks later, Jacky pulled to a stop in front of a man who stood with a husky on a leash. The husky was peeing on a car tire.

"Excuse me," Jacky said. The man looked over, raising his eyebrows.

"Have you seen a little terrier running around? He's black and has a white spot on his side."

Jacky pointed to her ribcage. Tim didn't point out that the guy couldn't see her gesture behind the door.

"Oh, *you* guys," the man said. "I've see you guys at the park over there. Your dog doesn't shut up, does he?" He laughed. "It's okay, Kit here doesn't, either. Do you, girl?" He patted the dog.

"Sure," Jacky said.

"No, I haven't seen him. What's he go by?"

"Jonas."

"Funny name for a dog," the man said. "You need something different, not a human name. It makes it better."

"Yeah, because Kit is *so* much better," Tim said to his window.

"I'll remember that next time," Jacky said.

"You guys have a number, just in case? Kit loves the cold, so who am I to deny her?"

Jacky rattled off her number, the man nodding with each digit. After a quick "thanks," Jacky put the car in drive and continued the search.

"Why aren't you looking?" she asked. They were stopped at a light and she was squinting at the cemetery next to them. Like she was trying to find the ghost of their relationship, Tim thought.

"I am," Tim said. "I'm just tired." He slouched, resting his head on the seatbelt.

"You're drunk."

"I *was* drunk," he said. "You woke me up."

Jacky sighed. "Keep looking."

Outside a school, Jacky asked a group of kids if they had seen Jonas. Most wore shorts and one held a soccer ball. Tim thought about his favorite shorts—his sleeping shorts. He hadn't been wearing them for his nap that day because the drunkenness had snuck up on him, but he fully intended to put them on when they got home. He'd lie back down on the couch under a few fleece blankets and let the rest of his Sunday melt away like ice cubes in a glass of Svedka.

The kids knew nothing and Jacky kept driving. They circled back around to their block. Tim thought they were done, that Jacky was giving up. He thought she was being nice for a change. He thought maybe she'd let him go take a nap. They'd look again later. She hit the brakes early, though. They weren't parked in their usual spot under the tree.

"I think I saw Jonas," she said. "It looked like he was back by those garbage cans. Go look."

Tim sat, nodding and not looking at her.

"Damn it, Tim. I said go look."

She slapped his shoulder as she reached across her own body to point to a clump of blue garbage cans.

"I didn't see anything," Tim said as the locks click. Jacky turned to face him. The car idled. Jacky cocked her head and raised her eyebrows.

"Go," she said.

Tim pushed the door open with his boot and got out, stretching. He walked around the front of the car (suppressing the thought that Jacky might take her foot off the brake) and tiptoed across patches of ice to the cans.

He called for Jonas as he moved, alternating whistles and cheek clicks. He didn't see the dog anywhere. When he got to the cans, he pushed one in an effort to make it seem like he was looking hard, like he cared. He knew Jonas wasn't there. He knew, even though the world wobbled, that he wouldn't see the dog. The dog was gone. The dog was gone because of him. The dog was probably *dead* because of him. He must not have clipped the leash right this time.

"Do you see Jonas?" Jacky yelled from the car. Desperation pulled at her words. She didn't need to yell, Tim thought. She was only seven, maybe eight feet away.

"No," Tim said over his shoulder. He tried to move another can and found it frozen to the ground. He looked down and saw iced-over wheels. He thought about the ice in his freezer down the block—the half-moons that seemed to cool his alcohol quicker than crushed ice. They were his relief when Jacky got to be too much. He loved her, but she still got to be too much at times. She was almost always yelling these days.

"Get away from my cans," a voice above Tim said. He looked up to see a woman, obese to the point of getting herself stuck in her own window, staring at him from the second floor.

"We're looking for a dog."

Tim squinted against the glare from the raised window. The reflected sunlight seemed to pierce through his eyes and into his brain.

"Those are my garbage cans, not dogs," the woman said. Her words were drowning in saliva.

"I know," Tim said. "We thought we saw him, though. We were just looking."

"There's nothing there. They're my cans. I wouldn't put a dog in there. That's cruel." The woman paused to catch her breath. "I'm not cruel. I own six cats and they're all fat and happy.

Tim didn't disbelieve a single word.

"Well, there's no dog, so we'll be going."

"Of course there's no dog," the woman said. "It's probably dead, anyway. It's freezing out."

Tim hoped Jacky hadn't heard that, but couldn't imagine how she would've missed it. The woman was yelling. The whole neighborhood could hear.

Tim nodded at the trashcans, like he was thanking them for something, and went back to the car. Jacky had rolled the windows up and was blasting the heat. Her nose and cheeks were florid. She sniffled every few seconds. She didn't say anything about the woman. Tim was glad for that, glad for not having to talk about what would happen if they found a frozen Jonas.

"Tell me why," she said, speaking slowly. "Jonas is gone. Why did you leave him outside? Why didn't you—if you hate him that much—and I know you do—why didn't you at least make sure he was secure and freezing and not just fucking freezing?"

Her tone, Tim thought, matched the weather. Nothing but ice.

"I don't know," Tim said.

He remembered the PBRs. He'd drained three in his twenty-minute shower-and-change routine after his shift at the Cumberland Farms. Then he'd finished the six-pack and started another while making grilled cheese. Jonas had begged and pawed at his shin, waiting for food to drop. He remembered Jonas smacking the bells by the back door. The stairwell was always dark because the landlord cared about light bulbs as much as Tim cared about sobriety. Tim had followed Jonas down and opened the screen door for the dog. He thought he'd hooked Jonas to the stake in the yard, but his memory was snowy.

"You don't know? How could you not know?" Jacky asked. She then laughed one of her sarcastic laughs, one that announced to everyone that she already knew the punch line.

She turned down another street and pulled over, leaving the car running. Heat fogged the windows, spreading like a puddle.

"You make it seem like it's a problem that I have a couple beers after I get home from the job that I go to every morning at five A-fucking-M," Tim said.

Jacky turned to face him. Tim shuffled to do the same.

"It *is* a problem, Tim," Jacky said. She had her palms up in a show of *no shit, Sherlock*, fingers splayed like she was the ten-time champion of arguing. "You make it seem like you have it so damn bad there. You sell coffee to the migrant workers and gas to those with real jobs."

"Is that what this is about?" Tim asked. He could feel his drunk burning off. "I told you, I'm working on it."

"Yeah, you are. Sure."

"You know it's been tough."

"I love you and all, you know I really, really do," Jacky said, "but maybe you shouldn't be blowing the money you make on weed and beer."

"Shouldn't we be looking for Jonas?" Tim asked.

"No. You opened this up, so we're going to talk about it."

"I didn't open anything," Tim said.

"You mean like a beer bottle?"

"So what the hell exactly are we talking about here?"

"Everything, Tim. Or nothing. Does it really matter? I do everything around here." She took a moment to pinch the bridge of her nose and sigh. "No, sorry, I don't do the drinking. You're great at that. Too bad you couldn't have gotten a BA in that."

Too bad, Tim thought.

"I told you. I'm trying to find a job," he said. "Good for you, you have a full-time job at the clinic. You test piss. Woo-hoo, Mom must be so proud."

"Fuck you," Jacky said.

                          GOD IN NEON

"You wish," Tim said. "You know why I don't wish that, too? Because you creep me the hell out when you try and talk sexy. It isn't sexy. It's weird."

Jacky's eyes widened for a moment before shrinking to slits. Her lips moved, but she didn't speak. Tim saw her hand twitch. Her nostrils flared with every breath.

"We should be looking for Jonas, he could be cold," Tim said, smugness lacquering his words.

"*You* should. You lost him."

Jacky pulled out of the parking spot and began driving down one of the major arteries of Manchester. Tim scanned every black lump, every piece of garbage that could've been the mutt.

They'd driven two miles away—Tim knew the distance from the days that running mattered—when Jacky slammed on the brakes.

"What?" he asked. Jacky pointed out the window. Next to the dirty brick wall of a pizza restaurant was a pile of snow with what looked to be a tail sticking out of it. The tail was black and nubby. Tim's stomach dropped. When he looked back at her, Jacky was biting her lip and scratching her cheek.

"Go look," she said. Her voice shook just a little, like Tim's hands did when he hadn't had a drink for a few hours. Jacky pulled into a parking space and turned the heat up. "Go."

Tim sighed. There was no way to get out of this. He un-buckled himself and pushed the door open with his foot. Wind and loose snow whipped around and hit him in the face. He cursed under his breath and hauled himself onto the sidewalk, feeling his weight move like he was underwater. He stared at the tail. How could she have even seen it? It was barely two inches long and could've just been a rock.

It was not a rock. Tim knew that. He wanted it to be, but that part of your gut that reacted before your brain had done so, lighting a fire and twisting just like when he'd figured out his parents were getting divorced before they said so. They'd never taken him to Chuckie Cheese together like that.

Jacky had leaned over and pulled the door closed. She had her hands crossed over her chest and her eyes locked on Tim. He flicked his gaze to the door and saw that it had locked behind him. He sighed. Tim shoved his hands in his pockets and walked over to the tail. His first thought was to kick it—that was what he'd always done when he'd found a dead animal as a kid; he'd kicked it. Or, if he'd had a stick, he'd poked it. There were no sticks here, though; even if there had been, he could already here Jacky yelling about it.

Tim squatted. It was a tail all right. It didn't look familiar, but how often did you stare at your own dog's tail? He touched the tip of it, but his hands were numb and he couldn't tell if it was warm. He figured it wasn't, looking at the three-foot-tall pile of snow on top of the dog. He stuck his hands into the pile and began to pull the snow away. After a minute, Tim stopped to look around. He could only imagine what people were thinking. He probably looked like just another crazy, homeless person. Over his shoulder, he could see Jacky watching. He turned back and continued to dig.

A few more scoops of snow gone and Tim could see it was a dog, but it wasn't Jonas. His heart sank, not for the dog, but for the fact that his job wasn't over yet. He'd have to be out here more, longer. The dog's eyes were open and Tim turned away while he put a hand over the dog's face and tried to rub the eyes closed with a numb hand. It didn't work, and when he turned back the dog was still staring into the last space it would ever occupy.

What was he going to do? It wasn't Jonas. Jonas was probably in this same position somewhere else in the city. He'd have to stay out here, looking, freezing the entire time. And for what? Another dead dog? Wasn't one enough?

Tim stood and walked to Jacky's window. He decided to try something. He had no idea if it would work, but he had nothing left to lose.

Jacky rolled down the window, eyes large as they stared up at him. She looked to Tim like a child, waiting to hear if her stuffed animal had made it through surgery okay.

Tim lowered his head. A sob cracked the air between them.

"I'm sorry," Tim said.

Jacky was crying now. She made a move to unbuckle her seatbelt.

"No," Tim said. "Don't. I mean, I don't want you to see him. Let me take care of it. Let me bury him and then you can come pay your respects."

Jacky didn't say anything for a minute, then unzipped her jacket and handed it through the window.

"You'll need this," she said. She sniffled, "make it somewhere nice, like the park down the block. No one will be there right now."

"Okay," he said. "Yeah, okay. The park."

Tim thought about the liquor store next to the park. "I'll take him. You go home."

Jacky nodded. She then grabbed his hand and kissed it. Her lips were warm and it felt like fire. He couldn't remember the last time she'd done that. He couldn't remember the last time she'd done anything even borderline romantic. Tim let his hand hang in the space between them. Somewhere, something that had settled below all the alcohol in him told him he needed to tell her the truth. He shook his head.

"I love you," Jacky said, and she meant it.

"I love you, too," Tim said.

A moment later, Jacky drove off. Tim turned to the dog. He wasn't going to bury it in the park. No. He'd earned some love and affection and all he had to do was cover the dog again. It'd never occurred to him how easy it was to lie to Jacky. He didn't, usually, but this? This was a revelation, like the first real snowmelt in March. By the time this snow melted, someone else would take care of the dog. He'd need to make a cross or something for Jonas, but he could do that later.

Tim kicked snow over the dog, making sure the tail was not visible. When that was done, he walked down to the liquor store where he bought a pint of Old Crow. The clerk was someone he knew from the local bars; they chatted for a minute. There was no one else around, so Tim cracked the top and raised it, catching eyes with the clerk. This one was for Jonas, he thought, wherever he was.

WELCOME TO MILWAUKEE

Dave told me he needed help on a project and I was the only one he trusted. He said there would be pizza, but asked me to bring beer.

"Don't tell me this is some sort of murder-suicide thing," I had joked. He didn't laugh.

"Just get over here," he said.

On the way to his house, I stopped and grabbed a case of High Life. The door was unlocked when I got there; a sticky note told me to meet him upstairs. Dave still lived in his parents' house—in the basement—and we used to spend a good amount of our time there stoned, staring at the feet that passed by on the sidewalk outside the basement window. When we were teens, we'd play this game where we guessed the person's entire life story based on just their shoes. Dave had always seemed better at it. The game had limped on through college, happening less and less until finally, when I got my job, it had stopped completely.

Somewhere upstairs, Dave's Labrador, Panther, barked and I followed the noise. Panther circled the ladder that led up to the roof like he was trying to find a good place to sit. When he saw me, he came over and gave my leg a hump. It was our thing—that's what I told Dave's parents whenever it happened in front of them.

"Don't worry," I'd say. "It's consensual."

They were Lutheran and didn't appreciate the joke.

The hatch was open, so I climbed up, cradling the case of beer at my side. Dave stood on the edge of the roof holding a piece of paper, staring down at it. There was no pizza to speak of.

If he heard me, he didn't acknowledge me, so I cracked two beers and walked over. He looked up when a beer can filled his vision

"Hey," he said.

"There's no pizza. You said there'd be pizza."

"Pizza's gonna come," he said. "Chill out. We'll work a bit first."

I sighed and took a drink. It was only eleven-thirty, but it seemed like a fine idea. I worked for a marketing firm and had just gotten back from a trip to Seattle. It was my first day off in almost two weeks, I didn't care when I started drinking.

Dave handed me the paper. There was a grid pattern marked off in pencil and the words *Welcome To Milwaukee* written in the boxes in pen. He'd spelled Milwaukee wrong and had crossed out the wrong letter. It looked like a botched kid's crossword.

"What's this?" I asked, handing him back the paper.

"It's our project."

"Let me rephrase. *Why* is this our project?"

"We're painting it on the roof."

"This roof?" I looked around. I saw a faint chalk outline on some of the shingles.

"Yes, this roof." Dave tilted his head, finished his beer, and grabbed another.

"Why?"

"For the planes."

I raised an eyebrow. Dave had odd ideas from time to time—he had it in his mind until he was twelve that a raccoon would be a good pet—but this seemed a category all its own.

"We're in Minneapolis. You know that, right?"

"I know," he said.

We spent the better part of a six-pack getting ready to paint. He'd lugged a few paint cans up already, but there were still more in the basement. He'd apparently been buying them from a guy at the hardware store in the same plaza as his father's mechanic shop.

"They fell off the truck," Dave told me as I passed two cans up to him on the ladder. He set them down and grabbed another two

GOD IN NEON

from me. None of the cans looked dented, but I still hoped he wasn't getting scammed too badly.

I was a little drunk by the time we'd gotten everything to the roof; I thought about what it would feel like to fall off. I asked Dave about it—he said not to worry. He spoke slowly and in a measured way like he'd tried it before.

"You may break a bone or two, but you won't die. My father told me my grandpop fell off this roof when he was thirty and only broke a couple ribs."

"A couple ribs," I said, thinking of food.

Dave handed me a paintbrush. I felt artistic, standing up there, staring out over the river.

"Where do you want to start?" he asked.

"Milwaukee," I said.

He nodded and clapped me on the shoulder. "You got it, bud."

He'd pulled a replica of the design from his pocket and handed it to me.

"Start on the E and we'll meet in the middle."

I nodded. Dave picked up some of the empties and walked to the edge of the roof, looking down. I watched him lean over, one eye closed, in profile, concentrating like he was throwing a dart. He dropped a beer can and it clattered off the asphalt. Dave leaned over more. I waited for the moment that he'd drop, just be gone from view. I wondered if he'd yell, if there would be any sign other than his body not being there.

I wondered how often he did this.

"I missed," he said. "I hate missing." He grabbed another can and aimed again. This time we heard the *tink* of metal on metal.

"Bingo," he said, pumping an arm. Dave kept leaning over, staring.

"Back up, dude," I said. He waved an arm in my direction.

"I'm fine," he said. "I like this."

I'd made it to the K when Dave abruptly stopped talking about the latest project he was working on down at the shop. I looked up. Dave stood, staring at a black dot. A plane was heading for us, growing by the minute. I went to say something, but Dave shushed me. When the plane got closer, close enough to see the company's logo and the row of windows—windows that looked like raisins from where we were—Dave began to wave. He waved for three minutes, until the plane had passed over us and, I assumed, made its way to MSP.

"Can they see you?"

Dave shrugged.

I didn't know what to say to that. I didn't know how to tell him that it was a stupid idea to wave to a plane. I'd done it once—on vacation in Florida—and my father had told me it was a waste of time.

"Do you think anyone on that plane will want to see *you*, of all people, as they get ready to land?" he'd asked me. I was seven, at the time, in a pool, and he was sitting nearby with a bottle of Jack somewhat following my mother's orders to make sure I didn't drown.

"Yes," I said.

"Well, they don't. They want to see their loved ones, or a new place. If they're on vacation, they want something new. They want a sense of adventure. Not some spoiled pale kid in a pool."

Twenty minutes later, another quarter of the whiskey was gone, and my father reported that it was time to go back to the hotel room.

Dave had gone back to work. He'd about finished the first word before I'd made it halfway through mine.

"Why not Minneapolis?" I asked. The better part of the case was gone and I was having a hard time holding onto the brush. I had to focus to keep a hold of it, and I had to squint to read the map. The sun, high above us like a sentinel, did not help.

"That seemed too boring," Dave said. "I want people to wake up when they get here. To live a little."

"I see."

"You know how it is, man. There's stuff here, but there isn't *stuff*. It isn't like Chicago or L.A. or New York. It's Minneapolis, a city that's mostly known for being a twin. It isn't even good enough to be known on its own."

He slapped a shingle with an open palm. "Why would people want to come here? This way, if someone's dozing on their way from, I don't know, Terra Haute or Boston or something, and the ride's been just fine this'll get their heart going."

"That seems mean," I said.

I wasn't paying much attention and had idly begun to paint a line of ants trooping across the middle of the U. I looked up at Dave, but he didn't seem to notice. I tried to wipe it away with my hand, which only served the make the letter look even worse.

"It isn't, man. Think about it."

I waited for him to continue, but realized after a minute of silence that he really *did* want me to think about it.

"I've thought about it," I said. "I've got nothing."

Dave stood and walked over to me. He had a crumpled beer can in his hand, which he tossed off the side of the roof, not aiming this time.

"I'm making people live."

"What if it's, like, a grandfather with a weak heart?" I tapped my chest.

Dave waved my words away like he was clearing away candle smoke.

We had just about finished when Dave got a call. His father, he told me after. There had been a wreck on 94 and he was going to have to stay late to start repairs.

"Big money client," Dave said, rubbing his fingers together in my face. His father had built up his grandfather's business and they were known as some of the best mechanics in town. Dave had worked there since he was sixteen—eight years, now—and would take over when his father decided to let him. He'd changed my oil on every car I'd ever had. Dave got two days off a week. His father usually took one.

"It doesn't matter that he's the owner," Dave told me once, when he was drunk. "That fucker would rather be there than here. He wants me to do the same. He says if I don't, he's not going to let me have the business. He's going to cut me off completely. He says I can't let the family down like that."

Dave had closed his phone and was sitting on the edge of the roof, legs dangling. I sat next to him, my knuckles turning white as I gripped shingles. Dave didn't sway or wobble. His eyes were on the horizon. We sat mostly in silence, drinking. After a minute, Dave began to kick his legs and lean forward a bit. He still had a grip on the edge of the roof, but he moved like there was a heavy breeze. He said nothing, just rocked. And I watched.

The smell of paint mixed with that of the evergreens in the yard. The aroma reminded me of cleanser, of freshness. I waited a few more minutes before speaking.

"You still haven't told me why," I said. "Like, *really* why you're doing this."

"Because," Dave said. "Because it helps me get away. When I see a plane coming, just for a second I can pretend I'm anywhere that isn't here. Even if it's just Milwaukee."

He looked up. In the distance, a bird became a plane, the engine drone preceding it on the light breeze. He stood.

"You know what it's like to know that you're never going to leave the city you grew up in?" He pointed a beer can at me, looked down at it, then pulled it back to his lips. Dave tilted his head back and drained it before tossing it off the roof.

"You don't because you leave every other goddamn week."

I didn't say anything. What could I say?

"Exactly. You get the hell out and see the rest of the country. Coming back here is relaxing to you. You get to sleep in your own bed, eat your own food, masturbate in your own shower."

"I can't help that man. It's my job to be on the road."

"Yeah. I know. And my job? My job is to get oil on my jeans every goddamn day in the same goddamn shop in the same goddamn strip mall that my dad did, that my grandfather did. You think I want that? Why do you think I *still* have that world map on my wall?"

I hadn't thought of the map in years. Dave was always telling stories about the pastel-colored countries that hung there when I hung out with him as a kid. The stories were always adventures, and he was always the hero.

Dave huffed. He picked up the last beer, opened it, and drained it in one long swallow. The plane was closer now, louder; I watched Dave's eyes lock on it as it approached.

"You can go somewhere. Take a vacation sometime, get out of town. Your dad will allow that."

Dave laughed. He broke off his staring contest with the plane's belly to lean over the edge again.

"Man," I said. I held a hand out. "Stop doing that."

Dave looked at it and spit off the roof. The empty can followed soon after.

I saw *Mueller and Son* becoming *Mueller and Son and Son*. I saw Dave's hands covered in oil and grime, not entirely clean until they give him one last sponge bath before embalming him. I saw the furthest place he'd ever go, a long weekend trip to a convention in Fargo. I saw everything he did when he looked up at the planes.

Dave resumed his position. The plane was almost upon us, its shadow floating over the land in front of us like a spectral whale. Dave's hands were on his hips and he squinted against the sun. His eyes reminded me of marbles. I looked up at the plane, wishing desperately that the map would stay up forever, that he'd keep telling stories. I wished for nothing more than having one person— one—look down and get scared, that their heart would beat into their throat and that they would have to look at their itinerary, just to make sure.

COURTSHIP

was up by five that morning, freezing from a night in my car in a Bismarck parking lot. My blankets were vacuum-packed and stuffed between a box of canned ravioli and a space heater in my trunk. Honestly, every muscle in my back and neck felt vacuum-packed.

I stood outside the Cracker Barrel until six when I was greeted with a "Come inside, you poor dear, coffee is almost ready" through the still-locked doors. I washed my face and armpits in the sink, ate egg whites and toast, and drank a pot of coffee. I didn't have to tell the waitress what I was doing or where I was going like I had in Fargo or Stillwater or Baraboo. I was out and back on the highway by seven-fifteen. I had less than a day to cross Montana, drop the car off in Missoula and start my life. Then I had to find the job I told my parents I already had.

I hit the Montana line at ten-to-ten and pulled off at Exit 1. My first glimpse of Big Sky Country, where I'd live for the next half-decade, was a sign that read *Welcome to Beef Country* painted in cow's-blood-red, ushering me into downtown Wibaux. Three bars and four storefronts faced off in a duel across the main street. The bars' windows were the only ones that weren't clouded, like they had gone blind and had been left to die. I chose the third bar, the Wibaux Inne. I wondered what the extra E was for as I pushed the door open.

A game show blared from a television in the corner and three men sagged over the bar. The bartender, a bison of a man, leaned against the inside rail. The wood of the bar was dull and scarred.

There were photos in plastic frames and license plates tacked to the walls. The bar stools looked rusted in place. From the TV, Bob called someone on down.

"What can I get you?" the bartender asked. He swung a towel in slow circles using one hand. It looked like a flag of surrender, like the last bit of fight had left him decades ago.

I read off one of the taps. He nodded and poured, using a letter opener to scrape foam off the top. It hung like shaving cream from the blade for a moment before he flicked it into a garbage can, where it landed with a sound like rain on a tent. The bartender spun a cardboard coaster along the bar and placed the glass down in front of me. The beer was something local and had the color of all the fields I had spent days driving past—the ones I'd pulled over next to and pissed in because no one was there to stop me. The three other men at the bar had bottles of Budweiser. The man closest to me had wrapped a napkin wrapped around his and it clung to the condensation, fluttering like a crippled butterfly under the air vent.

I sipped and watched. The men seemed to want nothing to do with me and I was okay with that. I played with my phone. I felt drops of sweat slide down my ribcage. I could've drank faster and been out of there, but I didn't. I sipped and watched.

In the time it took me to drink one beer, the other three had downed two more each. When done, they raised their fingers like they were checking the breeze and the bartender pulled more beer out of the ice chest. The sound of bottles opening seemed like an indictment against talking. The man sitting furthest from me watched the game show, an elbow resting on the bar and his head lolling back. The man in the middle looked to be sleep-drinking. His nails were the color of dead leaves and, from my seat, I could see cracks near the ends of them.

"Another?" the bartender asked.

I didn't need another, but didn't want to be back on the road. Hundreds of miles of straight and flat can suck the life out of anyone. Even the GPS eventually stopped talking.

"Where you from?" he asked as he took my glass and poured, cutting the foam again. I wondered why the beer was so foamy. I wondered if he was a bad bartender or if it even mattered out here.

"Jersey," I said.

He raised an eyebrow. "You don't sound like it."

One of the other men agreed.

"Say coffee," the bartender said.

I said it. I didn't yawn across the vowel like most people I knew.

"My dad's from Minnesota," I said.

"You don't sound like that, either," the nearest man said.

"Why you out here?"

I told them I was heading west, for a job or more school or whatever I could find. I told them between sips that I had been hired to drive a car and that I needed to cross the state in less than a day.

"Good thing cops out here don't care," the bartender said. "What's your name?"

I introduced myself, half-standing on my bar stool to lean over and shake Roger-the-bartender's hand. Up close, I could see tobacco stains in his beard. He introduced Earl, Jim, and Jackson. Each main raised his beer at the sound of his own name.

"I'll get this next round," Earl said.

He pulled a ten out of his pocket and let it float onto the bar. Roger slid it off and put it in the open till behind him. Taking a stack of coasters, he placed one behind each of our drinks. I looked at the coaster.

"A place marker," Roger said, moving to clean glasses.

"So you're going to school, huh?" Jim said. He sat up, began to wobble, and grabbed the edge of the bar with both hands.

"Maybe," I said. I sipped and thought about things like yeast and hops and how I shouldn't have another. About how I needed to drive six hundred more miles.

"Whatcha going to study?" Jim had swiveled in his seat to face me. Earl leaned back a little when he did so.

"Not sure," I said.

"What about forestry? I hear they have a good program out there. My daughter Jessie—sweet Jessie—she tells me that."

Jim stopped talking for a moment and sat up straighter. He looked like a prairie dog sighting coyotes. Two beers had already soaked through my light breakfast and I wanted to be the one to scare those coyotes away for him.

"Forestry?"

"Let me ask Jessie," Jim said. "Let me ask her. She's home. I can ask her." His consonants slurred. He asked Roger for the phone.

"You know I can't let you keeping calling people from here," Roger said. He leaned forward, hovering over Jim like a thunderhead.

I looked down at his hands. They were covered in white hairs and the skin ballooned around the knuckles looking ready to burst.

Earl had finished his beer and, without looking. Roger dug another out of the chest. He pawed the empty back and let it fall into a garbage can. The sound of glass on glass was jarring, like Roger wanted to wake us up a bit.

"Just once more," Jim said. He folded his hands in prayer and looked up at Roger, who reached behind him and grabbed the phone off its cradle. He asked for the number.

"It's the one I wrote down last time."

Roger said something under his breath, turned around and flipped a few papers that were tacked to a board with broken corkscrews.

"Can't you just tell me?" Roger asked.

Jim rattled of a few numbers—paired and out of the usual phone number rhythm. He said he wasn't sure. The phone looked to be older than I was and had a cord. It was the creamy color of forgotten book pages.

I was halfway through my beer and I knew I should be getting back on the road. Money was contingent upon time and I had little of either. These men, lost in the necks of their bottles, seemed okay, but it wasn't a place to stop. I could come back, maybe, if I needed to.

I drained my beer and said the next round was on me. Roger, who had handed the phone to Jim, nodded.

"You aren't much at all like someone from New Jersey," he said. I watched the phone cord pulse above the bar. Jim's hand shook as he held it, sending more tremors. I thought of the sea and waves and how I wouldn't see them for a while. I thought of the old phone my family used to have, hidden behind a picture frame in the wall. It had the same curled cord. As a kid, I always wanted to bite it.

Earl raised his bottle at me. He finished his beer, put the empty near the edge of the bar and held his hand open for the next.

"Mighty kind," he said.

Jackson, as he got his next beer, asked for a round of the house special. Roger blinked and pressed his lips together momentarily before he spoke.

"You sure about that?"

"Yeah, I trust him," he said, looking sidelong at me.

I thought about what he could possibly trust me with. Roger nodded. He bent over with a hand on his back and a groan. He came back up with a Jack Daniels bottle. An envelope had been tape to the bottle. Roger showed me the words *Special Brew* written in Sharpie.

"Jackson here got a little bored one winter. Decided to make a still. Got this."

Roger poured shots and replaced the bottle. It was the color of honey. Jackson pointed at the shot, then, Jim, then the phone, then the shot.

We were waiting.

Jim, after talking to someone who may have been his wife, had his daughter on the line. I could hear the buzz of a female voice on the other end. He told her to come down to the bar a few times, repeated that there was a nice boy from Jersey who was going to the U and that she needed to meet him. Toward the end of the conversation, his sentences began to get cut short. His words tumbling down the side of a mountain. A minute later, he handed the phone back.

"She said she just woke up." Jim held his beer in both hands, choking it.

Earl, who had been quiet, seemingly mesmerized by the prizes on the television, burped.

"You know she ain't coming," he said, lifting his shot glass. The rest of us followed, draining them. I coughed and they said nothing.

"But she should. We've got a new friend and he doesn't even seem like he's from the East. He could be from here, if he had some cowboy boots."

I didn't tell them I'd bought a pair of boots in a store outside Vegas the year before. They were in the car. It didn't seem relevant that I'd been planning this escape for a year.

"You know, you could marry her if you wanted," Jim said. He leveled his bottle at me and sighted like it was a rifle.

I looked down at the foam stuck to the inside of my glass. Through it, I saw someone had carved the name Bruce into the bar.

"She doesn't have a man, and she's studying. She'll be smart—*is* smart," Jim said. He looked like he was going to stand up and had his hands on the bar to push off, but thought better of it.

Jackson laughed. "Ain't hard to be smart in this town."

Jim spun on his stool. "Does that matter? No. She goes to the U. She's going to be something." He turned to me. "She can be your wife."

I wasn't sure what to say. I wasn't looking for a wife, but I wasn't *not*, either. The last girl I'd been with had dumped me in Pittsburgh outside her family home. While we'd been breaking up, her dog kept running at the invisible fence, getting shocked back onto his ass, and doing it again. She told me she didn't want to do distance. Dating a cowboy wasn't in her life plans. I'd tried to tell her that not everyone in Montana was a cowboy and that Missoula was an artsy town, but she'd shut me up with a quick kiss, leaving a peppermint tingle on my lips longer than she'd bothered to stand in her driveway watching me.

Jim spun back. "We live on a farm outside town. She knows how to ride horses and milk cows."

"I'm not really looking for anything," I said.

"You sure?" Earl asked. "She's been the belle of the ball here since she was little. Grown up into a nice, beautiful lady." His smile was predatory.

"What is she studying?" I asked.

"Art," Jim said. "She always wanted to be a painter. First time she had a calf for showing at the fair, she named it Rembrandt."

Roger refilled my beer. I wasn't sure who was paying for this one, but I didn't say no. It seemed like it would be wrong to say no.

"You like art?" Jim asked.

"Sure."

"She went there because Missoula is great for artists. Lots of those types out there. Must be the mountains."

I thought about the images of the mountains I had seen, how they broke into the skyline like brass knuckles.

"How old is she?" I asked. If she was going to show up, I figured I should at least know a little bit about this girl. We were heading the same way. We could always meet up later and grab drinks or bison burgers.

"Twenty-one. She's got one more year, but she wants to stay out there. Hates it here." He took a drink, coughed. I imagined the beer bubbles rising up in the back of his throat and tickling the space behind his nose. "She's never said it, but I ain't stupid."

I saw his eyes lock on the phone then float back toward me.

"So it's nice out there?" I asked. "I've never been."

I wondered about the winters and snowshoes and how close Montana was to the tundra.

"Beautiful," Roger said. "Used to hunt up near Glacier."

I nodded. We spent the next fifteen minutes not talking. Roger bought a round and joined us in a drink. My stack of coasters grew. There was something very European about it. I picked them up and dropped them in a stack like poker chips. They fell without the satisfying clacks.

"I'm getting hungry," Earl said. He was tapping his hands to the beat of a car commercial jingle on the TV.

"Still an hour until the specials at Speedy Pizza start," Roger said.

Roger was looking up and over the bar, staring like he had just seen the Virgin Mary. I turned and saw a clock that had been made of a cross-section of tree, deer antlers for arms, and house numbers screwed in place.

"You going to be around in an hour? Speedy's got the best pizza in town," Roger said.

"It's the only pizza," Jim said.

For the next hour, we drank.

At twelve, Roger ordered. I tossed a five on the bar and he shook his head.

"Don't worry about it," he said.

Jim told Roger to call his daughter back and tell her it was time for pizza. That would get her to come down.

"If she comes, you can marry her," he said. I looked at him. His eyes were foggy and probably had been for years. His upper lip shook when he wasn't speaking. I saw razor cuts around his mouth and stray hairs near his Adam's apple. He smiled at me and I saw gaps and decay. I wondered if Wibaux had done the same thing to Jessie.

"Hey," Jim said after I didn't respond. "There's a picture of her here. You can see her. You can see she's good enough to marry."

He stood and walked the wall, running his hand along it like a blind man. I could just make out the sounds of him talking to himself. Earl shook his head.

I heard Jim make a sound. A moment later he dropped a picture that had been glued to a slice of cardboard in front of me.

It was a photo from a pageant, Ms. Ski Fest, from a few years before.

Jim looked the same. He had his arm around a girl, whose head stopped at his nose. She was redheaded and smiling. She wore a tiara and a sash. Someone playing an accordion was bisected by the edge of the photo.

"Ski Fest," Roger said. "Like Polski. Adamski, Kowalski, Polaski."

"Ski, ski, ski," Jackson said.

"Ah," I said.

"Most beautiful Ms. Ski Fest in decades," Jim said. "Since her momma."

I didn't say anything, just nodded. I agreed. Her picture set me at ease. It was easy to focus solely on her in that photo. There was the way Vaseline made sunlight erupt from her smile and the way her hip canted to the side. She looked confident, and that was more than I could say for anyone else I had dated. Or even myself.

I gave him a half-smile and handed the photo back.

"So, are you going to marry her?"

Jim was looking down at the photo again, rubbing his thumb over the other woman in the photo, on Jessie's other side, His thumb blotted out her entire head and shoulders.

"I've never met her," I said. I found it hard to believe it would be that easy. I knew, somewhere in my mind, that it wouldn't be, but part of me wanted to think it could be. *Would* be. I'd be able to sit back and tell my parents I found a job, a place to live, and a wife.

"You will," Jim said. "She'll be here. She loves pizza. Remember that. Pizza." He said it slowly, like I had never graduated college. Or completed first grade.

"When will the pizza be here?" Earl asked.

Roger was about to speak when there was a noise outside, like someone stumbling through a tool shed. There was metal on metal and the sound of things snapping. Everyone sat up straighter. Roger was already moving out from behind the bar to the door by the time the men and I were working our way into standing position. I put my feet on the ground and felt my body wobble. I leaned on the bar. I imagined all the blood rushing back through my body, like standing up straight had let the glow go unbroken from head to heart to feet. I imagined my legs like kinked hoses that had been untangled. There was a red river and I saw it moving through me, carrying all the beer to the furthest outposts of myself.

My eyeballs felt heavy as I finally pushed off the bar. I wanted to close my eyes, as if that would ease the pressure, but it just made the world spin. I saw light through my eyelids and it felt like it was moving in circles in front of me. I imagined gauze and the need to push through it. It felt thick around my eyebrows and behind my ears. I became keenly aware of a ringing sound.

The others were already outside when I finally made it to the door. Earl had his beer in hand and was sipping it, like there wasn't a car crashed into the utility pole across the street.

Roger was on a cell phone and Jackson and Jim stood on the curb, leaning their torsos out over the street as if they couldn't leave the sidewalk. Jim atonally sang, "What the fuck?" Roger closed the phone and began to cross the street. When Jim took a step off the curb. Roger turned and barked at him to stay.

I stood with my back against the door. I could feel the metal bar pressing into my spine. It was warm through my t-shirt. I felt grounded standing there. If I pressed against the door, I didn't sway. I didn't need to make decisions about my life. I wasn't worried about how I'd get to Missoula by sunset or about the payment that would allow me to rent a room and buy groceries. I thought about Jessie. I wondered if she was the pizza delivery person they were trying to extricate from the car. I wondered if I would ever get to meet her. It occurred to me that I didn't know Jim's last name and I wouldn't even be able to look her up.

I closed my eyes and rubbed them with my palms. Television static exploded across my eyelids. The ringing in my ears persisted and seemed to mesh with the light patterns. I thought about how if I stayed in Wibaux, I could get married. I could settle down on a farm and raise kids and calves and that seemed all right. I thought about telling my parents I married a beauty queen. I thought about how I could get the new job opening at Speedy Pizza.

Nearby, I heard shouting. A siren buzzed somewhere. I heard something about a dog. I felt pebbles press into the bottoms of my sandals. It was hot, and that was not helping my developing headache. It was another minute before I realized my eyes were still closed. I opened them and my vision was cloudy. A blink re-aligned my contacts. Everyone stared at the wreck. Glass glittered like treasure on the asphalt. I looked down the street at my own car. It was blue and stuck out amongst the rusted trucks. I took a step sideways. My ankle rolled and I pressed a hand to the glass storefront to steady myself.

I couldn't stay here. If I stayed, I'd have to take that pizza job and marry Jessie. I'd be a cowboy and a farmer and I wasn't ready for that.

I made it to my car and no one said anything. I couldn't remember if I paid my tab, but I wasn't too bothered. What were a few beers between strangers? I opened the door and was hit with a blast of sweat-smelling hot air. I collapsed across the front seat, hitting a rib on the gearshift. It would hurt in a little while. But it didn't bother me for now. Warmth spread from the point of contact. I realized the door was open and pulled it closed with my foot. I heard a muted click. It wasn't shut tight, but it was shut.

GOD IN NEON

ACKNOWLEDGMENTS

Thanks to: Alan and Michelle Slaughter, Katie and Tom Hickey, Marya Barry, Ted Wheeler, Steph Post, Mark Powell, Kenny Lane, Nick Sweeney, Taylor Brown, Lynn and Wayne Barry, the Sundress Academy for the Arts, Sean Taylor, and There Will Be Words.

I'd also like to thank the publications in which some of these stories were first published.

"God in Neon" first appeared in *The Heavy Contortionists*.

"Burying the Johnboat" first appeared in *Fried Chicken and Coffee*.

"A Shot for Father Stephen" first appeared in *Deep Water Literary Journal*.

"The Dead Rabbits Society" first appeared in *Queen Mob's Teahouse*.

"Fame in the Graveyard" first appeared in *The Circus Book*.

"Frozen Jonas" first appeared published in *Drunk Monkeys*.

"Welcome to Milwaukee" first appeared in *Midwestern Gothic*.

"Courtship" first appeared in *Four Chambers*.

ABOUT THE AUTHOR

Sam Slaughter is the author of the chapbook *When You Cross That Line* and the collection *God in Neon*. His work has appeared in places such as *McSweeney's Internet Tendency*, *Midwestern Gothic*, and *Atticus Review*. He lives in Columbia, SC where he works as a spirits writer for *The Manual*. He can be found online at www.samslaughterthewriter.com and @slaughterwrites.